ADVENTURES OF THE
LITTLE WOODEN
HORSE

KINGFISHER CLASSICS

ADVENTURES OF THE LITTLE WOODEN HORSE
URSULA MORAY WILLIAMS
ILLUSTRATED BY PAUL HOWARD

BLACK BEAUTY
ANNA SEWELL
ILLUSTRATED BY IAN ANDREW

GOBBOLINO THE WITCH'S CAT
URSULA MORAY WILLIAMS
ILLUSTRATED BY PAUL HOWARD

HEIDI
JOHANNA SPYRI
ILLUSTRATED BY ANGELO RINALDI

MILLY-MOLLY-MANDY STORIES
JOYCE LANKESTER BRISLEY
ILLUSTRATED BY JOYCE LANKESTER BRISLEY

TEDDY ROBINSON STORIES
JOAN G. ROBINSON
ILLUSTRATED BY JOAN G. ROBINSON

THE ADVENTURES OF TOM SAWYER
MARK TWAIN
ILLUSTRATED BY CLAIRE FLETCHER

THE CALL OF THE WILD
JACK LONDON
ILLUSTRATED BY ANDREW DAVIDSON

THE SECRET GARDEN
FRANCES HODGSON BURNETT
ILLUSTRATED BY JASON COCKCROFT

TREASURE ISLAND
ROBERT LOUIS STEVENSON
ILLUSTRATED BY JOHN LAWRENCE

URSULA MORAY WILLIAMS

ADVENTURES OF THE LITTLE WOODEN HORSE

ILLUSTRATED BY
PAUL HOWARD

FOREWORD BY
VIVIAN FRENCH

KINGFISHER

Publishers' Note
The Publishers have used the first edition of *Adventures of the Little Wooden Horse*, published in Great Britain in 1938 by George G. Harrap & Co. Limited, for this publication. It is reproduced here complete and unabridged.

KINGFISHER
An imprint of Kingfisher Publications Plc
New Penderel House, 283-288 High Holborn,
London WC1V 7HZ
www.kingfisherpub.com

First published by George G. Harrap & Co. Limited in 1938
First published in hardback by Kingfisher 2001
This edition published by Kingfisher 2005
10 9 8 7 6 5 4 3 2 1

A CIP catalogue record for this book is available from the British Library.

ISBN-13: 978 0 7534 1207 7
ISBN-10: 0 7534 1207 1

Printed in India
1TR/THOM/FR(MA)/115INDWF/F

To

CONRAD SOUTHEY JOHN

CONTENTS

FOREWORD   9

1   THE LITTLE WOODEN HORSE   13

2   UNCLE PEDER IN TROUBLE   19

3   THE LITTLE WOODEN HORSE SELLS HIMSELF   25

4   THE LITTLE OLD WOMAN AND UNCLE PEDER   33

5   THE LITTLE WOODEN HORSE
    SEEKS HIS FORTUNE   42

6   THE ESCAPE FROM FARMER MAX   54

7   THE LITTLE WOODEN HORSE GOES TO SEA   66

8   THE LITTLE WOODEN HORSE
    GOES DOWN THE MINE   73

9   THE LITTLE WOODEN HORSE SEES THE KING   85

10 THE LITTLE WOODEN HORSE RUNS A RACE   100

11 THE BLACKSMITH AND HIS SON   120

12 THE LITTLE WOODEN HORSE AT THE CIRCUS   129

13 IN THE NURSERY   140

14 THE SWIM TO THE SEA   160

15 BLACK JAKEY   168

16   THE LITTLE WOODEN HORSE
     SWIMS THE OCEAN   184

17   PIRATE JACKY AND BILL BLACKPATCH   211

18   THE LITTLE WOODEN HORSE GOES HOME   227

19   THE LITTLE WOODEN HORSE
     GOES TO A WEDDING   242

     AUTHOR NOTE   254

FOREWORD

I HAVE ALWAYS LOVED the story *Adventures of the Little Wooden Horse*. I think it must have been my father who first read it to me when I was very young, and I asked to hear it over and over again. I can clearly remember a friend complaining that when she came to stay she always had to listen to "that toy horse story" . . . and then she insisted on borrowing my copy of the book so that she could read it for herself!

As a child, the quiet little horse who had no particular wish for adventure had a truly magical fascination for me; he was my ideal hero. All too many of the books that were read to me starred big bold boys or clever feisty girls – characters that were not in the least bit like me. The little wooden horse was different; when you read the story you'll find out, as I did, that he is strong – but he isn't invincible. His paint fades, his wheels wear out and fall off, and he often needs mending. What's more, he is never boastful, or looking to find fame and glory. He has an endearingly simple innocence; all he wants is to be able to earn enough money so that he can return to his beloved Uncle Peder. He sets out into the big wide world all on his own. He does not have a companion to travel with, although he makes many friends along the way. He survives kidnap and servitude, good times and bad with a gentle astonishment that such things can happen to a quiet little horse . . . and he remains steadfast throughout.

When I grew up and had daughters of my own – feisty, clever, big and bold – I found to my surprise that they wanted to hear about the little wooden horse too . . . over and over again. I had thought that in our world of television, computers and razzle-dazzle books, the story of a wooden horse would appear old-fashioned, but I was wrong. There's a timeless fairy tale quality to the telling; even though it was first published in 1938, the story is as attractive now as it always has been. Why? Perhaps it's the clear voice of a true storyteller, a storyteller who knows exactly how to keep the reader gripped. Each chapter ends with a breath-holding new problem or situation; how can we not read on just a little more to see what happens? And then a little more . . . and then another chapter. Maybe it's the humanity of the little horse. Even if he is made out of wood, and his head comes off, he has a huge heart. Sometimes he feels sad and lonely, and sometimes he feels that he will never win through – but always he thinks the best of whoever he meets, and he does his best with a cheerful fortitude. Even when things are at their very darkest, he does not grow angry; he bears his lot with patience and hope.

As for his adventures – well! There has to be something here to catch the imagination of everyone, whatever their interests. There's a glorious mishmash combination of canals and barges, elephants and coal mines, kings and princesses – let alone the circus, the treasure island and the desperate swim across the ocean! When I read this story to my youngest daughter, we had several late nights because she couldn't bear me to stop . . . and, if I'm truthful, I didn't want to. It's the most wonderful story to read out loud and bears any amount of repetition.

The final attraction of this book for me has always been the relationship between the little wooden horse and Uncle Peder. It's a story about loving and being loved; the little horse has no ambition to travel and have adventures, but he will do anything to save his beloved master . . . and throughout his ups and downs, his one determination is that he will return home with enough of a fortune so that Uncle Peder never has to work again. Everyone longs both to give and receive such love, and this must be one of the main reasons why the story has such a never-ending appeal . . . and why I hesitate every time I pass a toy shop window. I'm still looking for my very own little wooden horse . . .

Vivian French

Bristol, 2001

1 THE LITTLE WOODEN HORSE

ONE DAY UNCLE PEDER made a little wooden horse. This was not at all an extraordinary thing, for Uncle Peder made toys every day of his life, but oh, this was such a brave little horse, so gay and splendid on his four green wheels, so proud and dashing with his red saddle and blue stripes! Uncle Peder had never made so fine a little horse before.

"I shall ask five shillings for this little wooden horse!" he cried.

What was his surprise when he saw large tears trickling down the newly painted face of the little wooden horse.

"Don't do that!" said Uncle Peder. "Your paint will run. And what is there to cry about? Do you want more spots on your sides? Do you wish for bigger wheels? Do you creak? Are you stiff? Aren't your stripes broad enough? Upon my word I can see nothing to cry about! I shall certainly sell you for five shillings!"

But the tears still ran down the newly painted cheeks of the little wooden horse, till at last Uncle Peder lost patience. He picked him up and threw him on the pile of wooden toys he meant to sell in the morning. The little wooden horse said nothing at all, but went on crying. When night came and the toys slept in the sack under Uncle Peder's chair the tears were still running down the cheeks of the little wooden horse.

In the morning Uncle Peder picked up the sack and set out to sell his toys.

At every village he came to the children ran out to meet him, crying, "Here's Uncle Peder! Here's Uncle Peder come to sell his wooden toys!"

Then out of the cottages came the mothers and the fathers, the grandpas and the grandmas, the uncles and the aunts, the elder cousins and the godparents, to see what Uncle Peder had to sell.

The children who had birthdays were very

"Upon my word I can see nothing to cry about!"

fortunate: they had the best toys given to them, and could choose what they would like to have. The children who had been good in school were lucky too. Their godparents bought them wooden pencil-boxes and rulers and paper-cutters, like grown-up people. The little ones had puppets, dolls, marionettes, and tops. Uncle Peder had made them all, painting the dolls in red and yellow, the tops in blue, scarlet, and green. When the children had finished choosing, their mothers, fathers, grandpas, grandmas, uncles, aunts, elder cousins, and godparents sent them home, saying, "Now let's hear no more of you for another year!" Then they stayed behind to gossip with old Peder, who brought them news from the other villages he had passed by on his way.

Nobody bought the little wooden horse, for nobody had five shillings to spend. The fathers and the mothers, the grandpas and the grandmas, the uncles and the aunts, the elder cousins, and the godparents, all shook their heads, saying, "Five shillings! Well, that's too much! Won't you take any less, Uncle Peder?"

But Uncle Peder would not take a penny less.

"You see, I have never made such a fine little horse before," he said.

All the while the tears ran down the nose of the little wooden horse, who looked very sad indeed, so that when Uncle Peder was alone once more he asked him, "Tell me, my little wooden horse, what is there to cry about? Have I driven the nails crookedly into your legs? Don't you like your nice green wheels and your bright blue stripes? What is there to cry about, I'd like to know?"

At last the little wooden horse made a great effort and sobbed out, "Oh, master, I don't want to leave you! I'm a quiet little horse, I don't want to be sold. I want to stay with you for ever and ever. I shouldn't cost much to keep, master. Just a little bit of paint now and then; perhaps a little oil in my wheels once a year. I'll serve you faithfully, master, if only you won't sell me for five shillings. I'm a quiet little horse, I am, and the thought of going out into the wide world breaks my heart. Let me stay with you here, master – oh, do!"

Uncle Peder scratched his head as he looked in surprise at his little wooden horse.

"Well," he said, "that's a funny thing to cry about! Most of my toys want to go out into the wide world. Still, as nobody wants to give five shillings for you, and you have such a melancholy expression, you can stop with me for the present, and maybe I won't get rid of you after all."

When Uncle Peder said this the little wooden horse stopped crying at once, and galloped three times round in a circle.

"Why, you're a gay fellow after all!" said Uncle Peder, as the little wooden horse kicked his legs in the air, so that the four green wheels spun round and round.

"Who would have thought it?" said Uncle Peder.

2 UNCLE PEDER IN TROUBLE

UNCLE PEDER and the little wooden horse became great friends. Everywhere that Uncle Peder went the little wooden horse went too, carrying the sack of toys on his red-painted saddle, so that Uncle Peder no longer walked with a stoop under his heavy burden, but upright, like a young man. The little wooden horse was useful in other ways too. He carried all the money. Uncle Peder just unscrewed his head and popped the coins down the hole in his neck, so that they were quite safe; and the little wooden horse was very proud of being so useful to Uncle Peder. He trundled along bravely as they walked from village to village.

"How lucky I am!" thought the little wooden horse, who was as happy as the day was long.

But the day came when no children ran out to meet them as they entered a village.

"How can this be?" said Uncle Peder, walking down the street. "Can they be in school?"

But it was not school-time, and there were children playing by the river. Why didn't they come shouting to Uncle Peder as they used to do? Why didn't their mothers and fathers, their grandpas and grandmas, their uncles and aunties, their elder cousins and their godparents, come out to ask the news: "Uncle Peder, Uncle Peder, what's happening there, up the valley? Now, Uncle Peder, tell us all about it!"

Nobody came out of the houses; not a child left the river to welcome Uncle Peder.

"This is very strange," said Uncle Peder, trudging down the street, with the little wooden horse behind him. Suddenly he came upon something lying in the road. It was the head of a china doll.

Uncle Peder stopped and picked it up. He shook his head as he looked at it.

"*I* never made such a doll," said Uncle Peder,

shaking his head again. "China face, silk hair – no! My dolls don't break either."

The poor broken doll lay in Uncle Peder's hand, with its yellow hair curled about his fingers. Uncle Peder looked more puzzled than ever.

A little farther on they found a broken steam engine, made of tin. Uncle Peder shook his head over that too.

"I never made toys of tin," he said to the little wooden horse.

Then he found a sheet of newspaper drifting about the village street that told him all about it. Of course nobody came out to hear his news if they already had a newspaper to read it in; and the newspaper told Uncle Peder that big shops had been opened in the town nearby, full of cheap toys. There the mothers and fathers, the grandpas and the grandmas, the uncles and the aunties, the elder cousins and the godparents, could buy all the playthings they wanted for the children, without waiting till Uncle Peder came round with his sack; and they paid much less money in the town for the cheap toys that broke than they paid Uncle Peder for his strong wooden ones. But the cheap toys were very pretty, and the children did not want Uncle Peder's any more.

Uncle Peder and the little wooden horse went on from village to village and found the same state of affairs. Nobody wanted Uncle Peder's toys now that they had new, cheap ones from the town. They didn't want his news either. No, thank you! They read all they wanted in the newspapers.

This was all very well, but Uncle Peder had to eat, and to pay for his food. One by one the coins disappeared as they came out of the neck of the little wooden horse. One day there were no more left at all.

"What shall we do, master?" said the little wooden horse.

"I must sell my toys cheaper," said Uncle Peder. And he sold his beautiful wooden toys for fourpence, twopence, and even a penny, along the high road. Presently the sack was empty, and the little wooden horse had nothing left to carry at all.

"What shall we do now, master?" said the little wooden horse.

. . . they found a broken steam engine, made of tin.

"Why, I'll sell my coat!" said Uncle Peder.

He sold his coat, and soon he was shivering, while his shoes let in the wet.

"What use are shoes with holes in them?" said Uncle Peder. So he sold those too; but the money soon went.

Now they were in a bad way. No toys, no money, no coat, no shoes, no paint on the little wooden horse, no food, and Uncle Peder shivering and aching all over!

"Master is ill," said the little wooden horse. "I'll go and sell myself."

So when they had settled themselves in a barn for the night, and Uncle Peder had fallen into an uneasy sleep, the little wooden horse trundled out into the moonlight and away on his little wooden wheels as fast as he could go.

3 THE LITTLE WOODEN HORSE SELLS HIMSELF

THE LITTLE WOODEN HORSE remembered that once, a long while ago, as he trundled through a village at Uncle Peder's heels, a little girl, very beautifully dressed, had leaned out of the window of a big white house and cried, "Oh, what a pretty little wooden horse!"

No one came out: it was too fine a house to buy toys from a pedlar in the streets. But the little girl had liked him all the same.

The little wooden horse knew that he was not so handsome now as in those days. The paint had worn off his red saddle; his blue stripes were scratched and bare; his four green wheels had travelled so far they were nearly worn out; but he hoped that the little girl would not notice these things. Uncle Peder had not been able to afford to give him a coat of paint for a long, long time, so he did his best to brighten himself up a little at a stream before setting out on his long journey to the village where the little girl lived.

All night long he trundled through the forest and over the hills, till in the morning he found himself in the village, outside the big white house that he remembered so well. Everything was quiet and asleep. Not a maid stirred in the house, though down the village street the cows were being driven to pasture, and the sun was quite high.

The little wooden horse went round the house, wondering when someone would come and open the door, and if he should knock, or neigh, or kick the wall gently with his wooden wheels till somebody noticed him. He looked up at the windows: the curtains were drawn across. In one window the curtains were covered with rosebuds and tied with blue ribbon. "Those belong to the little girl," thought the little wooden horse.

Nobody appeared, so he trotted down the garden and found a large playhouse under some apple trees.

"That's where she plays," said the little wooden horse, going round and round the playhouse a great many times on his four green wooden wheels.

When he passed the door of the playhouse for the fifth time a gruff, horsy voice called out from inside, "Who goes there?"

The little wooden horse stood quite still with fright, his heart going *pit-a-pat! pit-a-pat!* inside his hollow wooden body. Then he saw that the door of the playhouse was open a chink, and a great spotted rocking horse was looking at him from inside.

"Come here!" neighed the spotted rocking horse, and because the little wooden horse was too afraid to do anything else he squeezed through the chink of the door and trundled into the playhouse. There he was, under the rocking horse's nose, feeling as small and as foolish as could be.

The rocking horse was a splendid fellow. He had a red saddle and bridle, with silver rosettes, and shining silver stirrups. He blew through his scarlet nostrils at the little wooden horse, and asked him how he dared to come into the little girl's garden and trundle round and round and round her playhouse.

The little wooden horse explained that he had come to sell himself. "A little while ago she admired me as I passed by with my master," he said humbly. "Now my master is ill and has no money left to buy food with, so I have come to see if she still admires me and would like to give my master five shillings to have me for her own."

"Five shillings!" roared the rocking horse. "What do you think she wants with a scratched, broken, cheap toy like you? Do you expect to come and live in her playhouse with *us*? Look round you and think again!"

The little wooden horse looked timidly round the playhouse, and thought he had never seen so many beautiful toys. Besides the spotted rocking horse, there were baby dolls and dolls' houses and teddy bears and toy ships, and bicycles and balls and games and books and bricks and pictures. They were all glaring at him in a very unfriendly manner.

"Do you expect to come and live with *us*?" they repeated.

"She has a real pony out of doors too," said the spotted rocking horse. "What can you imagine she would want with *you?*"

"Grind him to powder!" shouted a toy soldier, jumping angrily about. "Grind him to powder under your rockers, Dapple Grey!"

The rocking horse reared up on his great rockers as though he really meant to do as the toy soldier said, but the little wooden horse turned and made for the door as fast as his wheels would carry him. Just as he reached it the door was flung open, and in ran the little girl he had seen at the window, all gay with the morning, and wonderfully surprised to see the little wooden horse.

"Why, whoever are you?" she asked, with her blue eyes as round as the saucers in her dolls' tea set. "And *what* are you doing in my playhouse?"

All the angry toys tried to explain at once; the spotted rocking horse was galloping up and down in his excitement. But the little girl slammed the playhouse door in their faces and took the little wooden horse away to the low bough of an apple tree, where she sat down and took him in her lap.

"Now tell me all about yourself, you funny little wooden horse!" she said.

The little wooden horse told his story, and the tears ran down his face again as he thought of his poor sick master and how hard it was to leave him. When he had finished the little girl put her arms round his neck and hugged him.

"Oh, you poor little wooden horse!" she said. "I could never, never take you away from your master! But I will tell you what you must do. You must go back to him and ask him to make me a little wooden horse just like you, only quite new, and then my father will give him five shillings for it."

Then she loaded his back with good things from the kitchen and gave him fifty kisses before he trundled out through the gate and back through the forest to the barn where he had left Uncle Peder.

Oh, how tired he was when he came at last to the old building and whinnied for his master! It was night again, and his poor little green wheels creaked with weariness.

"Oh, you poor little wooden horse!"

"Uncle Peder! Uncle Peder!" whinnied the little wooden horse, to let Uncle Peder know that he was coming with food and good news besides. But nobody answered.

"Is my poor master too ill to hear me?" thought the little wooden horse, quickening his pace, though his legs ached and he was ready to fall asleep for a hundred hours. He hurried into the barn, across to the corner where he had left Uncle Peder sleeping.

The barn was empty! Uncle Peder had disappeared!

4 THE LITTLE OLD WOMAN
AND UNCLE PEDER

THE BARN BELONGED to a little old woman, very kind-hearted, but very apt to scold, so that people were rather afraid of her and left her alone.

One morning when she went into her barn to get hay for her cow what was her surprise to find in the corner poor sick Uncle Peder – so full of fever that he scarcely knew where he was, and so thirsty that he begged her over and over for a drink of water.

"Bless the man!" said the little old woman. She offered him water, and when he drank half a pailful she took him into her cottage and put him to bed in her best spare room, under her patchwork quilt that had a thousand patches in it, with no two of them quite alike. "And there you shall stay till you are well again!" said the little old woman, going into the kitchen to make him a milk pudding, for she felt quite sure that that was just the thing to cure Uncle Peder of his fever.

Uncle Peder was only too glad to lie in a comfortable bed, under a splendid patchwork quilt of a thousand patches. He looked at the gay colours, too ill to think of anything else at all, not even of his little wooden horse. There he stayed while the hours went by, and the milk pudding was made, and the little wooden horse came trundling back through the forest to find his master.

When he had searched the barn up and down and made quite sure that Uncle Peder was nowhere to be found the little wooden horse put his bundle down in a corner and went outside. His heart was beating *pit-a-pat! pit-a-pat!* with anxiety inside his hollow wooden body, for he could not think where Uncle Peder could be, nor what had become of him.

Then he saw the cottage belonging to the little old woman. Perhaps somebody there could help him.

The little wooden horse trundled up the garden

path and battered on the door with his wooden wheels, making a fearful din.

Now Uncle Peder had fallen asleep, and seeing him so peaceful the little old woman herself had gone upstairs to bed. When she heard the battering on the door she flew into a temper, for she thought it was bound to wake Uncle Peder. So she bounced to the window to see whom she could scold, and there on the doorstep was a little wooden horse.

The little old woman immediately thought that some children, late as it was, had been battering on her door and had run away, leaving their horse behind. She put on her slippers and rushed down the stairs, scolding under her breath. Then, before the little wooden horse could say a word, she picked him up and flung him far away into the forest.

Bang! went the door. *Bumpetty-bumpetty-bump!* went the little wooden horse, rolling over and over where he landed, while the stars turned a thousand somersaults about his head, and the tall forest trees seemed to leap about like tossed straws.

Presently the little wooden horse lay still. The stars were no longer spinning, the trees were quiet, and he was very, very bruised and sore. Only one thing stuck fast in his mind, while his wooden body still smarted and ached. When the little old woman opened the door he had seen behind her Uncle Peder's jacket and that hanging over a chair in front of the fire!

When he felt better the little wooden horse got up carefully, in case his legs were broken or he had lost a wheel – but, no, nothing so terrible had happened after all. He limped slowly back towards the cottage door, for he meant to explain who he was to the little old woman, and ask her to take him to Uncle Peder.

When she heard the battering on the door for the second time the little old woman flew downstairs in a terrible rage. She was rather deaf, and in any case she was far too angry to listen to what the little wooden horse had to say. This time she flung him with all her might into the ditch that ran round her garden, and then she locked and bolted the door and went back to bed.

The little wooden horse saw that it was of no use

. . . the stars turned a thousand somersaults about his head . . .

to batter on the door. When he had lain in the ditch for some time he crawled stiffly out and went back to the cottage, where he waited patiently under the window until morning, hoping to hear Uncle Peder's voice by and by.

Sure enough, before very long the little old woman got up and went in to see Uncle Peder.

"How are you this morning, Uncle Peder?"

"Better, I think, and thank you. Well, yes, I think I may say I am a little better."

"Is there anything you would like, Uncle Peder?"

"Well, yes, and thank you. I think I would like a drink of your beautiful cow's milk."

"Well, then, you shall have it," said the little old woman, going into the kitchen to fetch a bowl.

The little wooden horse did not at once call out to Uncle Peder, for he was afraid the little old woman would be angry if he made any noise. Instead he waited patiently under the window till she should open the door.

By and by the little old woman came out to rinse her bowl, and saw him directly.

"What!" she screamed. "Are you there again? This time I'll chop you up for firewood!"

But the axe was in the barn, and she had a bowl in one hand, so before the little wooden horse could say a word she seized him by the leg and sent him twisting, spinning, and turning high over the roof.

He flew past the swallows sitting in the eaves, past the pigeons perched on the thatch, past the starlings nesting in the chimney.

"Look!" they all twittered to one another. "Look at the flying horse!"

The little wooden horse landed *bump!* in the cabbage bed, and now he was bruised all over. "This is too much!" said the little wooden horse as he lay among the cabbages. But by and by, as he felt better, he decided that it was better to be flung over the roof and dropped into a cabbage bed, and bruised a little, than chopped up for firewood by an angry little old woman. He lay there wondering what to do for a long, long while.

Presently the little old woman came out of the cottage with a milk pail on her arm. She was going to milk her cow. The little wooden horse saw her trot along the path to the shed at the back of the barn. "Oh, if only my master would come to the door!" said the little wooden horse. "Once I find him all will be well. It's a funny world! Here I am, a quiet little horse who only wants to serve his master and stay by his side, flung into the forest, tossed into a ditch, hurled over the roof! Who knows what will happen to me next?"

Suddenly he had an idea. Perhaps the cottage door was open. If it was he could run in and see Uncle Peder while the little old woman was milking her cow. He scrambled out of the cabbage patch, with the earth still sticking to his four wooden wheels, and began to go *creak-creak-creak!* round the cottage towards the front door.

But when he was nearly there he heard a shout behind him. The little old woman had finished milking her cow and was chasing him, waving her pail of milk in one hand, the milking stool in the other.

The little wooden horse began to run as fast as his wheels would turn, for the cottage door was standing ajar, and if he could only get to Uncle Peder before the little old woman caught him he felt sure his master would explain everything, and all would be well.

Creak-creak-creak! His four wooden wheels were stiff with earth, but they turned like lightning as the little wooden horse galloped towards the cottage door.

Crash! The little old woman had dropped her milking stool so that she could run faster; she was coming up the garden path, her face red with anger and haste. *Crash!* The milk pail went too! The milk streamed across the grass, tickling the toes of the daisies and the marigolds, who didn't really like milk at all. And then, just as he was slipping in through the open door into the cottage, the little wooden horse felt himself seized from behind, while an angry voice cried, "Well, I *shall* cut you up this time and put you in my copper!" as the little old woman picked him up by one leg and carried him away to the barn.

5 THE LITTLE WOODEN HORSE SEEKS HIS FORTUNE

THE LITTLE WOODEN HORSE was more frightened than he had ever been in his life, particularly when the little old woman took down the axe that was hanging on the wall of the barn and set him down on the floor.

"Well, this is too bad!" said the little wooden horse. "Here am I, a quiet little horse, whose only wish is to serve my master, going to be chopped up for firewood and put in an old woman's copper!" And just as the little old woman raised the axe to split him in two he made a dash for the door, and was out in the forest before you could count five.

The axe sank deep into the floor, and there was the little old woman pulling and tugging to get it out so that she could run after the little wooden horse and chop him up for firewood.

The little wooden horse didn't stop to be caught this time. He saw that the cottage door was fast now, so he hurried away to hide among the trees, where the little old woman could not find him.

"Well, well!" panted the little wooden horse. "Now whatever on earth am I to do? Here am I, a quiet little horse, torn away from my master and sent out into the wide world alone!"

He sat down under a tree to think, for his four little wooden legs were trembling so violently that all his wheels rattled.

He knew he could not go back to the cottage, for his life was not safe there, and who knew how long he would have to wait until Uncle Peder was well again?

"And what shall we do then?" said the little wooden horse to himself. "No food, no money, once we have spent the money we get for the wooden horse my master will make for the little girl!" He wondered if he should go back to the little girl himself. But, no; it was a new horse that she had asked for, and the spotted rocking horse would grind him to powder.

"I must go and seek my fortune," said the little wooden horse.

He thought how splendid it would be to come back to Uncle Peder full of coins. He would take off his head and pour out the money through the hole in his neck. Then they would both be rich and happy, and Uncle Peder would only make toys for fun, and for poor children who had none.

"For I am strong, and a quiet little horse," said the little wooden horse. "I ought to make my fortune very quickly."

He looked sadly back at the cottage window behind which Uncle Peder lay in bed, and then trundled away through the forest to make his fortune.

The little wooden horse trundled through the forest for two days and two nights, and still he hadn't made his fortune. In fact, there was not a single coin inside his little wooden body, and nobody had spoken to him on the road. By and by he fell in with some men in blue smocks, leading four horses.

The little wooden horse tucked himself in beside the horses and asked where they were going, because he was very lonely with nobody to speak to, so far away from Uncle Peder, left behind in the forest.

"Why, we are going to help Farmer Max with his haymaking," said the horses. "We go round to all the farmers in turn with our masters."

"Do you earn a lot of money like that?" asked the little wooden horse.

"Our masters do," said the horses. "We get a good feed at midday and when we go home. After all, what is money to us?"

"Could I come and work too?" asked the little wooden horse, who wanted some money very badly.

All the horses laughed good-naturedly.

"Why, if you want to!" they said.

At Farmer Max's the men signed a paper agreeing to work for three days for Farmer Max and to accept the payment he offered them. They went up one by one to sign the paper. The little wooden horse followed them.

All the men roared with laughter when they saw the little wooden horse following them to sign the paper. Farmer Max laughed loudest of them all.

"Well, what do you want, my little wooden horse?" he asked, laughing through his great black beard.

"I want to work for three days for money, like the others," said the little wooden horse. "I am strong, and a quiet little horse. I can work very well."

At that Farmer Max laughed louder than ever, but he sent the little wooden horse into the fields with the horses and the other men, and the haymaking began.

The men soon stopped laughing when they saw how hard the little wooden horse could work – how he harnessed himself to the heaviest carts and helped the horses pull the biggest loads. Wherever the work was heaviest, there he was, pulling, loading, straining, doing his best, making the other horses look lazy beside him. All the while Farmer Max strode to and fro, shouting through his great black beard, not laughing now, but ordering the men on harshly, cracking his whip at the horses, telling everyone to work harder and do better. But most of all he shouted at the little wooden horse, who was working harder than anyone there.

At the end of the day the men led their horses home, but Farmer Max took the little wooden horse into one of his own stables and locked him in for the night.

The little wooden horse was so tired he fell asleep directly, dreaming of Uncle Peder and all the money he was going to get when the haymaking was over.

The next morning he was early in the fields. The other horses welcomed the little wooden horse, who helped them so bravely at the heaviest loads.

"Why doesn't Farmer Max use his own horses for the haymaking?" asked the little wooden horse at dinner-time.

"They are all so thin and poorly fed they aren't strong enough," the other horses told him. "It is cheaper for him to use us. Our masters don't like coming here, but it is only for three days, and the money is quite good."

At the end of the third day when the men lined up to get their money they patted and praised the little wooden horse, who was with them, waiting for his money too.

When he had paid the men Farmer Max burst out laughing again. "What does a little wooden horse want with money?" he said, and was going to put away his purse when the men stopped him.

"You must pay the little wooden horse!" they said angrily. "We don't know where he came from, but he worked better than any of our horses, and he must have his money too."

At that the farmer's eyes grew crafty.

"Look here, my little wooden horse," he said, "how would you like to stay on with me a little while and earn more money? I see you are a strong little horse, and a quiet one. I could find plenty of work for you on my farm."

The little wooden horse thanked Farmer Max, and said he would like to stay on for another week and earn some more money. So he said goodbye to the men and the other horses and stayed with Farmer Max.

For a whole week the little wooden horse worked as he had never worked before. Farmer Max kept him busy from morning till night, pulling such heavy loads that sometimes he was afraid his little wheels would come off. He went to bed so tired he could hardly dream, but he thought quite a lot about Uncle Peder and the wonderful surprise he was going to give him when the coins rolled out of his neck into Uncle Peder's lap.

At the end of the week he asked Farmer Max for his money; but Farmer Max said, "Well, now, my little wooden horse, how would you like to stay still another week since you work so well, and earn still some more money?"

The little wooden horse thought he would like to earn some more money, but the work was very hard and the days were long. Still, he agreed to stay another week with Farmer Max, who worked him harder than ever all day long, and locked him into a tumbledown stable at night.

At the end of the week he went to Farmer Max and asked for his money, but again the farmer asked him to stay another week. And so it went on, till the little wooden horse had worked six weeks for Farmer Max, but had never had a penny in payment, which troubled him very much, as he wanted to get a lot of money for Uncle Peder.

At last he went to the farmer and said he didn't want to work any longer, but would like to have his money and go away. Farmer Max roared with laughter, so long and so loudly that the little wooden horse grew angry, and although he was a quiet little horse, he stamped on the floor with his four little green wheels (now caked and muddy from the farm) and asked for his money at once.

Farmer Max then told the little wooden horse that he had never intended to give him a penny, but he wasn't going to lose him! Oh, no; he was far too good a worker! So he took him by the head and locked him up again in the tumbledown stable, where tears of anger ran down the nose of the little wooden horse as he thought of Uncle Peder and the money that would never be his.

Day after day Farmer Max drove the little wooden horse out at dawn and worked him till sunset. Night after night he locked him up and went away chuckling at the thought of all the hard work the little

Farmer Max kept him busy from morning till night . . . .

wooden horse was doing for nothing. He meant to keep him for ever and ever.

But although he was so tired by the end of the day that he could scarcely trundle home, the little wooden horse spent half his night making a hole in the back of his stable, for even if he could not get his money he meant to escape.

Every night he scrabbled and burrowed till the hole grew so large that he had to cover it with straw by day, and at last it was just big enough for a little wooden horse to squeeze through. He waited one more day, for he wanted to have a whole night to escape in, and go a long, long way from Farmer Max before anyone found out that he had disappeared.

All day long he worked his very hardest. "Tonight I shall be free!" said the little wooden horse to himself, over and over again. When they came to take him home he was so excited he could not wait to have the cart unharnessed, but set off down the hill to the farm with it clattering behind him.

"Whoa!" called the farmer's man angrily, but he had

to run quite fast to catch up with the little wooden horse, who was so eager to get to his stable.

But when he got there – oh, poor little wooden horse! Farmer Max himself had found the hole and nailed it up with boards!

6 THE ESCAPE FROM FARMER MAX

"I SHALL NEVER, NEVER ESCAPE!" thought the little wooden horse, as the tears ran down his face. "I shall have to work here for ever and ever, and, oh, what will happen to my poor master?"

By the morning despair had made him desperate, and although he was such a quiet little horse, no sooner had Farmer Max opened the door to lead him out into the fields than he charged out between his legs with a rattle of his wooden wheels, and sent the dishonest farmer sprawling. Out came the money from his pockets; silver coins rolled all over the yard; but the little wooden horse did not stop to pick any up, not even the wages he had earned – not he! While Farmer Max sprawled on the ground he scampered out of the yard with such a spinning of wheels that the stones jumped up off the road and peppered the ducks in the pond.

Nobody tried to stop him, and when Farmer Max struggled to his feet the little wooden horse was gone.

The angry farmer looked up and down the road in vain: there was nothing to be seen. He asked the ducks which way the little horse had gone, but they would not tell him. "Quaack! Quaack! Quaack!" they chuckled rudely, standing on their heads in the water and waving their feet disrespectfully at Farmer Max. At last he mounted his horse and galloped down the road.

"By hook or by crook I'll catch that little wooden horse!" cried Farmer Max, but although he galloped for nearly five miles, he never saw a sign of the little wooden horse, and had to come back empty-handed.

"Quaack! Quaack! Quaack!" laughed the ducks, standing on their heads in the pond, and waving their feet at the angry Farmer Max.

Meanwhile the little wooden horse was hiding in the fields, with his heart going *pit-a-pat! pit-a-pat!* inside his hollow wooden body. For a long time he did not move, but when he did there was a *clink!* and a silver coin fell off the little wooden stand that carried his wheels.

"Well, that is a piece of good luck!" said the little wooden horse, who thought he had lost all his wages. He took off his head and put the coin into the hole in his neck, where it made a pleasant clinking sound. Then he stayed as silent as a mouse until the sun went down.

"What shall I do now?" said the little wooden horse when he was once more on the road. "Shall I go back to Uncle Peder and take my silver coin? But a silver coin is quickly spent, and the little old woman may chop me up for firewood. I had better wait until I have made my fortune."

So he trundled along all through the night till he came to the canal.

Up and down the canal moved great barges laden with timber, barrels, and bales, while sunburned men and women and little sunburned children sat in the sun, chatting, calling out to other barges, or walking along the shore beside the horses that pulled the barges down towards the sea.

One of the barges was lying in close to the bank, and the barge people on her deck were sad and silent, sitting close together in a little group with no horse and no word for anybody. The little wooden horse did not like to see people so melancholy, and he was lonely with no one to speak to, so he trundled up the bank and said, "Good day!"

"It may well be a good day for you!" said one of the barge people. "Quite a good enough day for a little wooden horse, standing at his ease in the sun! But we have all these pit-props to take down to the sea, and to send across the water to the mines, and our horse is dead, so the barge can't move, and other barges will get there before we do, and sell their pit-props, so that we shall not be able to get rid of our own when once we get there."

This seemed a pity to the little wooden horse, so he said, "Well, look here, barge people! I am strong, and a quiet little horse. What will you give me to pull your barge down to the sea before any of the other barges?"

At that all the barge people burst out laughing, which made them look quite cheerful after all.

"Well, look here!" they cried. "If you pull our barge a mile we'll give you a penny. And for every mile that you pull it you shall have another penny. But if we get down to the sea before any of the other barges you shall have a silver coin."

To the little wooden horse this all sounded very delightful, and he could hardly wait until the barge people had fastened the rope round his neck and told him to start.

They soon stopped laughing when they saw how well he could pull.

"Look at that, now!" they said. "This little wooden horse will certainly pull us a mile!"

The great barge moved out into the stream, with the little wooden horse pulling and straining on the bank. When they had gone a mile the barge people threw a penny to the little wooden horse, who had now two coins chinking pleasantly inside his hollow wooden body.

Then they began to catch up with the other barges which were on their way to the sea, and as they came up with the first the barge people shouted, "Way, there! Way, there!" so that the people on the barge in front had hastily to unharness their own horse to let

"This little wooden horse will certainly pull us a mile!"

the little wooden horse and his barge go by. His barge was called the *Marguerita*, and on its decks the pit-props gleamed like great sticks of yellow candy.

Every mile that they passed the barge people threw another penny to the little wooden horse, and you may be sure they did not laugh at him any longer. The other barge people did not laugh either when they saw him coming, and heard the shout of "Way, there! Way, there!" from the deck of the *Marguerita*, which meant that they had hastily to unfasten the rope from their own horses and let the little wooden horse and his barge go by.

The day went on, and now the little wooden horse had overtaken all but three of the barges ahead of the *Marguerita*; they were only a few miles from the sea. But the three barges ahead, the *Daisy-Anne*, the *Elisabeth*, and the *Charlotte-Marie*, were the fastest on the canal. They were pulled by powerful horses, who made the little wooden horse look very small indeed. He could see them ahead now, like specks on the towpath, and he thought he would have to be content with bringing the *Marguerita* fourth to the sea, and getting the fourth best price for the pit-props.

Suddenly, a long way behind, the little wooden horse heard the *clop-clop-clopping* of a horse's hoofs coming along at a trot. At first he thought it must be one of the other barges hurrying to catch him up, but as it grew nearer and nearer his heart began to beat, and presently in spite of himself he turned round to see who was *clop-clop-clopping* behind along the towpath.

Not very far behind he saw a big figure trotting along on an old grey horse. It was Farmer Max! The farmer was still looking for his runaway wooden horse, and somebody on a barge at the canal's edge had told how he had seen the little horse, harnessed to a barge, going down towards the sea. Now Farmer Max was hot in pursuit: he meant to catch the little wooden horse and take him back to work on his farm.

The barge people were astonished when the *Marguerita* began to move through the water at a speed that raised little waves around her prow, while on the bank the little wooden horse was galloping after the *Elisabeth*, the *Daisy-Anne*, and the *Charlotte-Marie* as though he meant to overtake them within a mile or so. When they heard the angry farmer shouting behind them and guessed what the matter was they laughed at Farmer Max and cheered on the little wooden horse, who was galloping his hardest, with the coins going *clink-clink-clink!* inside his hollow wooden body and the great *Marguerita* ploughing through the water behind him.

"Way, there! Way, there!" shouted the barge people as they came up with the *Daisy-Anne*. The people of the *Daisy-Anne* were rather loth to unharness their horse and let the *Marguerita* by, for they were near the sea and thought they should remain in their proper order; but then they saw the galloping farmer, urging on his old grey horse that was steaming with heat and panting with the speed.

The people on the *Daisy-Anne* thought this was a great joke. They took the rope off their horse and let the little wooden horse gallop by, with the stones flying under his wheels. Behind him came Farmer Max, but now the barge people had roped up their horse again, and he had to pull in or fall headlong over it. When he had got by the *Marguerita* had nearly caught up with the *Elisabeth,* and the people on her decks were shouting, "Way, there! Way, there!" so that they could go by.

The little wooden horse was nearly dead with fatigue, but still his four little green wheels spun round and round, and he trundled down the towpath, with the *Marguerita* swinging along behind him.

The people on the *Elisabeth* cheered them on as they passed her, with only two miles between them and the sea, and the great *Charlotte-Marie* ahead, her decks piled with pit-props and crowded with people watching the race. The people on the *Charlotte-Marie* thought that the little wooden horse was trying to race *them*: they did not notice Farmer Max galloping along on his puffing horse, who, however much he was whipped, could go no faster, and was nearly spent.

The *Charlotte-Marie* wanted to be first in port, and was determined not to let the *Marguerita* pass her, so they whipped up their own horse, and the great barge began to move rapidly down the canal towards the sea.

"Oh, dear! Oh, dear!" thought the little wooden horse. "If the *Charlotte-Marie* gets first into port we shall have to wait outside until she has unloaded her pit-props, and while we are waiting Farmer Max will catch me, and all will be over." And he made an even greater effort to overtake the *Charlotte-Marie*, which was plunging ahead at a great pace.

His wheels felt unsteady; at any moment he feared one might come off, and if that happened, then everything was lost. But he galloped faster and faster.

Closer and closer they drew to the *Charlotte-Marie*. In vain the people on her deck urged their own horse to hurry: he had come a long way and was already doing his best. Behind them the barge people on the *Marguerita* were calling, "Way, there! Way, there!" while ahead of them, already in sight, was the entrance to the port. The people on the *Charlotte-Marie* pointed to it, begging the *Marguerita* to remain behind now, since they were already so close and it made very little difference to anyone who entered first or second. But even if the *Marguerita*'s crew had been willing the little wooden horse himself would not hold back. He could hear the farmer coming up fast behind, the mighty snorts of his horse seemed already to be whistling in his wooden ears, and the people on the *Charlotte-Marie* had only just time to free their horse before the *Marguerita* swung past them, almost at the gate of the port.

7 THE LITTLE WOODEN HORSE
GOES TO SEA

ONCE IN THE PORT, the barge people quickly took the rope off the little wooden horse's neck, and told him to run and hide himself until they had sold their pit-props, when they would come and pay him the rest of the money they owed him. They were so kind he knew he could trust them, so the little wooden horse trundled away to hide among the timber and the rigging till it should be safe for him to come out again.

Meanwhile Farmer Max had tied up his horse and was trying to get into the port; but as he had no passport everyone laughed at him and refused to open the gate. So presently he had to go to a hotel and buy food for his horse, before riding back to his farm as angry as a man could be.

The little wooden horse went to the far side of the port and watched the pit-props being lifted on to a ship – fifty at a time – by a large crane. Then, to his astonishment, an elephant who had been patiently standing at the side of the port with his keeper was also lifted into the air and swung across to the deck for all the world as though he weighed nothing at all.

"Well, that is very extraordinary!" said the little wooden horse, who had never seen such a strange sight in all his life. He was still standing and staring when the sailors noticed him and began laughing at him.

"Look at this funny little wooden horse staring at the crane! Well, my fine fellow, would you like a ride through the air for nothing?"

The little wooden horse did not know what to reply.

"Well," he said to himself, "here I am, a quiet little horse, with no particular wish for adventure, having won the race of all the barges to the port, and escaped from the axe of an angry old woman and the clutches of a wicked farmer – now I'm being offered a ride through the air, and who is to say whether the boards of a ship are not harder than a bed of cabbages? Still," thought the little wooden horse, "what did not hurt the elephant is hardly likely to hurt me." So he thanked the sailors, and told them that he would very much like a ride through the air if he might give them the trouble.

The sailors put two bands under his wooden body, and then the crane began to lift him.

Up, up, up! he went, far higher than he had ever dreamed of flying – higher than the old woman's roof, higher than the trees in the forest. He looked down on the port and saw the *Marguerita*, with the people on her deck busy unloading the pit-props. He saw the *Charlotte-Marie* waiting outside the port, with the *Elisabeth* close behind her. He saw no sign of Farmer Max, who had gone away to feed his horse, and this gave him a very pleasant feeling.

Now the crane began to set him down. Down, down, down! he came, like the swoop of a bird. The little wooden horse thought it was a delightful feeling as he came nearer and nearer to the deck of the ship. Then he saw that the crane was not going to set him down on the deck, but in a great hole in the boards which led down to the hold. Down, down! he went, till he felt his four little wheels gently touch the ground again, and there he was in a stall beside the elephant, under the deck.

They were both very surprised to see each other, and the little wooden horse had to tell his story a great many times before the elephant would believe him. After which, as the little wooden horse was very tired and sleepy, and the elephant's stall was quite comfortable, he curled himself up in the straw and went to sleep.

When he woke up there was a great deal of noise going on outside, and the little wooden horse decided to go and find the barge people. He asked the elephant to open the door with his great long trunk.

"But I can't open the door!" said the elephant. "Look how fast I am tied up! They won't let us out till we are across the sea!"

"But I don't want to go across the sea!" cried the little wooden horse in a great state of agitation when he thought of Uncle Peder lying ill in the forest, and the barge people of the *Marguerita* waiting to finish paying him and to give him the silver coin. "Do *you* want to go over the sea?" he asked the elephant.

"Of course I do!" said the elephant, quite surprised. "I'm going to join a circus, and I shall earn a lot of money and become very famous. Perhaps the King will come and see me, and the ten little Princes and Princesses, and I shall have my name painted up in red and gold on all the tents."

"That's all very well," said the little wooden horse. "But I'm a quiet little horse, and I don't want to become famous. I only want to stay beside my master, once I have made my fortune, and live happily ever after. I don't want *my* name written up in red and gold."

He began to batter on the door with his poor little worn wheels, but there was far too much noise going on outside for anyone to hear him. Before very long the ship began to move, and he battered harder than ever – but nobody came.

"You had far better be quiet and make the best of it," said the elephant. "After all, who knows? You may make your fortune very quickly across the sea."

They were both very surprised to see each other . . .

The little wooden horse sat down quietly, and began to think that perhaps after all the elephant was right. Across the sea there would be no Farmer Max to chase him, and he might be able to make a great deal of money. He lay down beside the elephant and made the best of it as he had been told to do.

Presently, however, the ship began to roll, and both the elephant and the little wooden horse were very seasick. They were most unhappy for three days and three nights, but then they came into another port, and that was the end of their voyage.

8 THE LITTLE WOODEN HORSE
GOES DOWN THE MINE

THE LITTLE WOODEN HORSE wondered what he should do next, as he waited with the elephant for the ship to be unloaded. He asked if the elephant thought a little wooden horse could earn money in a circus too.

"Well, no," said the elephant kindly. "You see, your paint is just a *little* spoiled and worn. And then you would have to sign on for several years, and I believe you are anxious to get home to your master."

"Oh, I am!" said the little wooden horse hastily, and he began to wonder what else he could do to make his fortune.

"Now, in the mines, where all these pit-props are going, I believe they use a great many horses," said the elephant. "Why don't you try and get work there?

If, as you say, you are strong, and a quiet little horse, I think you ought to be very successful."

The little wooden horse thought this over, and decided that the elephant's advice was good, so when at last the door opened and the elephant was taken out he trundled off to hide among the pit-props that were being taken off in great loads and put into a train.

After a long journey the little wooden horse found himself at a great mine. He was lonely and missed the elephant, for there were no horses to be seen about, for all that he had said. He crept away from the pit-props and went up to the nearest miner, a large fellow with a dirty face, whose eyes nearly popped out of his head when he saw the little wooden horse trundling along to meet him. When he heard what he had to say the miner put his hands on his hips and roared with laughter.

"Call the foreman!" he shouted. "Here's a little wooden horse come to find work in the mine and wants a shilling a day and his keep!"

Soon a little group of miners were gathered round

the little wooden horse, teasing him and asking for his story.

The little wooden horse did not like their loud voices and black, dirty hands, but he was a quiet little horse, so he answered them politely, and at last the foreman told the men to take him down the mine to the other ponies. So amid cheers and laughter the little wooden horse was put into a kind of black cage with nine or ten men, and lowered down an immense shaft into the mine.

They led him down dark passages to the stables where the ponies lived when they were not pulling the trucks. Here they left him all alone, wondering if he would ever see daylight and Uncle Peder again.

By and by the ponies were brought in for the night, while the miners went up to their homes in the village above. The little wooden horse kept very still in the corner of the stable, for a big black pony had been turned into the stall with him, and he was afraid to move.

But the black pony seemed to know he was there.

It snuffled all round the stable till it came to his corner, when it laid back its ears with an angry squeal.

"What's that?" squealed all the other ponies in the mine, throwing up their heads.

"Yes, what are you?" screamed the black pony angrily, as he nosed the little wooden horse all over. "And what are you doing here?"

"Oh, please! I'm only a very quiet little horse," explained the little wooden horse, as he tried to tell them his story. But the ponies were not at all pleased to see him.

"What do they want with a little wooden horse here?" they said. "Aren't we good enough?" And they sulked all night. In his corner the little wooden horse kept as still as a mouse, but he shivered and trembled with fear.

In the morning the other ponies were no more friendly than at first. They lost no opportunity of kicking and hustling him; and when they were led out to work and harnessed to the trucks they saw to it that the heaviest loads fell to his share, and that he made the longest journeys. But the little wooden horse worked bravely, for he had the thought of Uncle Peder to encourage him, and he knew that at the end of the week he would receive his money like the other miners, and by and by he would make his fortune.

The ponies were angrier than ever when the little wooden horse came back with his wages at the end of his first week in the mine. "*We* don't get any money!" they complained. "We only get kicks and blows!" Which was partly true, for they were a lazy lot of ponies, and they soon grew jealous of the way the little wooden horse was petted and praised by the foreman. So when Sunday came and the ponies were taken up for a scamper in the field above the mine they managed to leave the little wooden horse behind, and he had to spend a long, lonely day in the empty mine by himself.

This happened week after week, but the little wooden horse was patient; he spent the days counting up his money and wondering how soon he would have enough to take back to Uncle Peder.

One day he was working in a far corridor of the

mine with three other ponies and some miners. The day's work was nearly over, and the little wooden horse was glad, for the ponies had been laughing at him all day long, and he wanted to get back to the quiet corner of the stall where he slept.

"Your master would not know you now!" the ponies teased him. "Red saddle, blue stripes – all gone – all black as coal!"

The little wooden horse knew very well that his beauties were faded, and lately he had lost a wheel, so that he pulled the trucks along *cloppetty-clack! cloppetty-clack!* and even the kind-hearted miners smiled when they heard him coming.

"But when I have made my fortune," said the little wooden horse, "I shall have a new coat of paint, new wheels, a new red saddle, and three new blue stripes. One can't have everything at once."

The day's work was nearly over when there was a rumble in the mine, and all the miners stopped working to listen. The three ponies pricked up their ears.

"What was that?" asked the little wooden horse.

"That was an explosion. Didn't you know that?" the other ponies scoffed. "Part of the mine has fallen in somewhere."

"We had better go back," said the men, and they began to unharness the ponies.

The little wooden horse was hardly free before there was a tremendous explosion quite close to him, like a thousand peals of thunder.

"Run! Run!" he heard the men say, and in a moment things began to rattle about his wooden ears, as though the roof of the world were coming down – but it was only the roof of the mine they were in. The awful crashing went on, and the little wooden horse was knocked over and over, and flung about and battered, till at last he lay still under a pile of loose stones.

"This is a very strange thing," said the little wooden horse, as soon as he could hear himself speak. "Here am I, a quiet little horse that only asks to stay by his master's side, flung out into the wide world to seek my fortune, tossed across the sea, and now the roof of the world itself has come down on my head, and I shall never see my master again."

For the moment it seemed that the little wooden horse's words were true, for the explosion in the mine had brought a thousand tons of rocks down on his head, and there he was, shut in a tiny cave many fathoms beneath the daylight, a thousand miles from Uncle Peder.

Just at that moment he heard a movement beside him, and there lay the biggest of the ponies, with the two others close by, also knocked over by the explosion, but all alive and well, except that their noses and eyes were full of dust.

"What happened to the men?" asked the little wooden horse.

"I saw them run away," said the black pony. "I think they all ran to safety before the mine fell. But what is going to happen to us? We shall all die of thirst and starvation in this little hole."

But the little wooden horse was already busy exploring their prison. He pushed his little wooden head here, thrust his three remaining wooden wheels there, and hunted for a way to get out.

"I can smell fresh air," he said. "Somewhere there is a chink or a crack, and I'm going to find it."

The ponies watched him anxiously.

"Oh, do find a way out, dear little wooden horse!" they begged him humbly now. "If you do we will never bite you or kick you again. We were jealous and unkind, and we treated you badly, but we will never be so wicked again if you will only find a way to take us once more up into the sweet yellow sunshine."

At last the little wooden horse discovered a cranny through which the cooler air of the outer mine was blowing, and he became so excited that he thrust his head far through the crack and could not draw it back again. Now here he was in a worse plight than before – half of him in the cave, blocked and wedged in by rocks, and half of him in the cool dark air outside, but quite unable to free himself.

Inside the hole the ponies seized him gently by the tail and pulled, but nothing could free the little wooden horse from his uncomfortable position.

"Pull harder! Pull harder!" he cried, till at last the ponies were pulling with all their strength.

Suddenly the head of the little wooden horse flew off and fell among the stones, and he was free at last – but headless! There lay his head on the wrong side of the cranny!

Now he had no head and only three wheels, but, nothing daunted, the little wooden horse flew at the cranny, battering and thundering at it until it was large enough for him to squeeze through and find his poor little wooden head. He did not notice that while he thundered and battered nearly all his wages flew out of the hole in his neck and were lost among the stones.

Now the little wooden horse thundered and battered harder than ever to make a hole large enough for the three ponies to squeeze through. He did not care that his last three wheels were chipped almost to fragments, and that the splinters were dropping off his once beautifully painted coat. Inside the cave the three ponies battered and hammered too with their hard little hoofs, till one by one they were able to squeeze through the cranny into the corridor of the mine. Then they galloped back as fast as their legs could carry them to the shaft, with the little wooden horse limping in the rear.

At the entrance to the mine the miners could

At last the little wooden horse discovered a cranny . . .

hardly believe their eyes when they saw them, for they had been quite certain that the ponies had been killed in the explosion. They took them straight up to the surface for a day's holiday in the sun, and with them went the little wooden horse.

When they had been shut into the field the three ponies galloped round and round, wild with joy at being safe and free again.

The little wooden horse stayed where he was, in a corner of the field, quite quiet and still. He crouched in the long grass while the hours went by, and the other ponies shrilled and gambolled. Now and then he shook his head to hear the three coins jingle that still remained in his little wooden body, but he did not nibble at the clover or roll in the sunshine. For a terrible thing had happened to the little wooden horse after all those weeks that he had been down in the mine. He had become quite blind.

9 THE LITTLE WOODEN HORSE
SEES THE KING

WHEN NIGHTFALL CAME the other pit ponies were taken back to the mine, but the little wooden horse was left behind. He crouched in his corner of the field, and for the first time for weeks heard the familiar night noises that he remembered in the forest where he had left Uncle Peder – the owls hooting, the twittering bats, the rustling foxes, the dry hissing of the hedgerow riddled by small brown mice.

When the sun rose he could feel it shining on his battered body, but for all he could see he might still have been in the darkness of the mine.

"Now I shall die," said the little wooden horse, "for I have no money and no eyes, and only three wheels. What use can I be to my dear master now?"

But before he could die he heard footsteps in

the grass, and two kind, warm little hands encircled his body.

"Oh! Oh!" said a kind, warm little voice. "What a *beautiful* little wooden horse!"

Now it was so long since the little wooden horse had been called beautiful that the surprise quite revived him, and he blinked his poor little blind eyes and decided not to die for the present. As he blinked it seemed to him that a ray of light darted across his eyes, as though he were not, after all, so blind as he had supposed!

The miner's little boy wrapped the little wooden horse in his blouse and took him back to the village. There he scrubbed him under the pump till his paint began to show again: a glimpse of his red saddle appeared under the coal dust, and presently his three blue stripes peeped out too. When his mane was brushed and combed the little wooden horse began to feel a new fellow, while little by little his poor eyes were recovering, till at last he could see the miner's little boy himself, and the little boy's mother, and his baby sister, and the spotlessly clean kitchen to which he had been brought.

In the evening the miner himself came home, and this was the best moment that the little wooden horse had known for many a day, for no sooner had he finished his supper than the boy's father brought out his pocket knife and cut four new wheels for the little wooden horse, which he fastened on with bright new nails. Then, while the little boy watched and admired – "with his mouth hanging open wide enough," said his mother, "to catch all the sharks in the bay" – the miner brought out a pot of red paint and a pot of blue, and painted up the little wooden horse till you would have said he had come straight out of Uncle Peder's sack that very night.

The little wooden horse and the miner's boy were so pleased they ran round and round the kitchen, waking up the baby sister, so that they both got a scolding from the little boy's mother, and the miner got a scolding too for making such a noisy pair of them. But on the whole everyone was very happy, and the evening passed pleasantly away.

The miner's boy and the little wooden horse soon became great friends. The little wooden horse thought no more about going back to work in the mine, for his coat was far too fine and fresh, and if he spoiled it, who would give him another? Then he did not want to become blind again, and the explosion in the mine had frightened him very much.

He still thought a great deal about Uncle Peder, on whose account the loss of his money troubled him very much.

The miner's boy soon found the last three coins that jingled about inside his wooden body. "What a splendid moneybox that would make!" said the miner's boy. So he took his own coins out of the red stocking his mother had given him to keep them in, and put them down the hole in the neck of the little wooden horse. His baby sister thought this made a good rattle; but, rattle or moneybox, the little wooden horse did not mind. He guarded the little boy's money carefully along with his own, and played with the baby sister all over the floor.

But the time came when he began to think once

more about seeking his fortune, so he was glad enough when one day the miner's boy said to him, "The days are pleasant enough, my little wooden horse, but it seems to me there's more in the world for you and me to see. All my life I have wanted a little wooden horse of my own, so that I could go to the city and see the King and the ten little Princes and Princesses. Then I should buy a beautiful present for my father, and for my mother, and for my baby sister, and ride back here to the mine with a sackful of cakes and surprises. Now that I have five silver coins of my own I really think we had better go, my little wooden horse."

The little wooden horse had nothing to say against this, for he asked for nothing better, so one morning the two of them rose before anyone was awake, and trundled up the long, long road towards the city, the miner's boy first, walking very fast because he was happy and felt a man, while behind him came the little wooden horse on his four new wooden wheels, wishing that Uncle Peder could see him with his fine newly painted saddle and three blue stripes.

On his back he carried the empty sack that the miner's boy meant to fill with cakes and presents when he went home.

"Perhaps I shall find some work to do in the city to get some more money," said the little wooden horse as he trundled along the long, long road behind the miner's little boy.

When at last they came to the city they found the streets thronged with people, standing, watching, waiting, but doing very little else, it seemed.

"Do the people always behave like this in the town?" the miner's little boy asked of a passer-by, for he was not used to seeing people so idle. At home it was his mother or in the mine his father and the other men, who were always bustling about and being busy. In the little boy's life nobody stood still. To the little wooden horse too it seemed very strange, although by now he had seen more of the world than the miner's little boy.

"Why, it's a holiday!" said the man, smiling kindly down at the miner's little boy and his wooden horse. "It's the King's birthday today, and he is going to drive all round the city with the Queen and the ten little Princes and Princesses in the royal coach driven by ten white horses. That's what we are all waiting to see!"

Now all his life the miner's little boy had been waiting to see the King and the Queen and the ten little Princes and Princesses, so he and the little wooden horse pushed themselves into the crowd to wait too until the procession should come along.

They waited and waited, but nobody came, and the people began to grow restless. They moved and craned and peered and shuffled, and although the miner's boy and the little wooden horse held tightly on to each other, they could not help being pushed and jostled about by the crowd, until presently they found themselves squeezed right to the back of all the people; and then they were jostled out altogether into a new road, with a hundred people between them and the road where the King must pass in his coach with the Queen and the ten little Princes and Princesses. But no coach came, and everyone was looking at one another and saying, "Where is the King? Where is the Queen? What can have happened to the royal coach and the ten little Princes and Princesses?"

"Oh, dear, how very unlucky we are!" said the miner's little boy, when they had been jostled right out of the crowd; and he wandered down the road in which they found themselves, too sad to mind where it led. The little wooden horse trundled at his heels, wondering if there were any fortunes to be made in a city already so full of people.

They had both lost heart, so they were quite taken by surprise when the road led them straight into the Palace yard. There, pulled up before the door, was the beautiful coach, drawn by ten – no, *nine* white horses, for the tenth stood by, held by a groom, its head drooping, great tears welling in its beautiful eyes, while a broken horseshoe lying on the cobbles showed at once what was the matter.

Beside the coach, on the Palace steps, stood the King and Queen and the ten little Princes and Princesses, as sad a royal family as could be imagined or seen, for it was quite clear that the nine white horses that were left could not pull the massive

. . . the road led them straight into the Palace yard.

coach alone, and some of the children would have to be left behind.

"We will try once more," said the King, looking anxiously at the great golden clock that towered over the Palace. "Take your places, children, behind your mother, and we will see if after all the horses can manage to pull us all."

The King and the Queen took their places; the royal footmen scrambled up at the back, for *they* could not be left behind; the little Princes helped their sisters into their seats, and climbed in themselves. All their little eyes sparkled, but their faces were anxious. *Could* the horses pull them all?

The grooms let go the heads of the nine white horses. Nine flashing manes tossed in the air, nine tails, white like floss silk, swished about their prancing legs, as with a mighty clatter and trampling the loyal creatures put their shoulders to the collar and heaved at the great coach. With a mighty effort they drew it a few feet over the cobbles, and then they came to a standstill, pawing the ground and shaking their heads, as though to say, "We have done our best!"

"They will never draw us all round the city," said the King. "And we are already twenty minutes late. We cannot disappoint the people. One at least of the children must remain behind, unless a tenth horse is brought within three minutes. You say you have inquired everywhere?"

"Everywhere, your Majesty," the grooms replied. "All the horses have gone into the country for the harvest."

The King now turned to his children, most of whom were in tears.

"Belinda, you must come: you and Ivor are the eldest. Helena, April, and Merlin had better come, and the twins: we cannot separate them. And Robin and Marigold: we promised them last year, and I will not break my word. Then, Madeleine, you are the youngest. You must stay behind."

The youngest Princess, with tears streaming down her cheeks (though she tried in vain to hide them in her pocket-handkerchief), stumbled out of the coach, and without a backward look at her luckier brothers and sisters fled up the stairs into the Palace. The

Princes and Princesses wept in sympathy, the Queen wiped a tear from her cheek, and the King gnawed at his moustache. The footmen and grooms might not show their feelings, but all the pleasure was gone out of their bearing; and as for the horses, they turned their heads mournfully towards the Palace entrance, and the sorrow in their beautiful eyes said plainly, "We did our best. *Please* don't blame us, dear Princess."

The coachman whipped up the horses, who strained once more at their golden harness, and the coach rumbled heavily across the cobbles towards the entrance to the yard. It had not rolled twenty yards before the horses came suddenly to a standstill.

"What is it now?" cried the King, who was getting impatient, while the youngest two remaining Princesses, at a look from their mamma, prepared to scramble down and follow their sister without further delay. But a footman who had run at once to the horses' heads now came running back to the King in some excitement.

"If you please, your Majesty, there's a strange little wooden horse has come into the yard from no one knows where, and he says can he take the place of your Majesty's tenth horse? He says he is a quiet little horse, and strong, and he thinks he may suit your Majesty well, and he's worked in the mines, your Majesty, and in the fields, and he can pull like any ten horses, he says."

"Harness him at once!" roared the King, for the hands of the golden clock pointed to the half-hour, and far off in the city he could hear the murmur of the people awaiting their King. So while the grooms rapidly harnessed the little wooden horse at the head of the nine white horses the eldest Prince ran indoors to tell his sister to dry her eyes and wash her face quickly, for she had to come after all. And while all the fuss was about the miner's little boy crept under the royal coach and clung to the axle like a little monkey, but he was seen by the groom, who brought him to the King, who told him to jump up behind with the footmen, for if his little wooden horse was as strong as he announced himself he could pull them all with ease. So all was smiles and laughter in the coach as the Princes and Princesses wiped their eyes and blew their noses and hugged their little sister, and the footmen sat up like two white candles, with the miner's boy between them, and the King smiled and the Queen smiled, and the horses sprang forward, led by the little wooden horse, the heavy wheels turning like windmills, for it was true that the little wooden horse knew how to pull.

Three times round the city they drove, while the people cheered themselves hoarse. They cheered the King, they cheered the Queen, they cheered the ten little Princes and Princesses. They cheered the nine white horses and the beautiful coach, spinning along as smoothly as silk, and over and over again they cheered "the King's little wooden horse" who led them all.

When at last they drove back to the Palace the King ordered the miner's boy and the little wooden horse to be comfortably housed in the kitchen apartments for as long as they liked to stay. Next day he would reward them both. Before they went indoors the youngest Princess ran and flung her arms round the neck of the little wooden horse.

"If it hadn't been for you I would have been left at home!" she said to him. "*Don't* go away at once! Let me see you again tomorrow, and the next day, and the next!" And she blew a hundred kisses down his little wooden ears before her elder sisters called her indoors.

10 THE LITTLE WOODEN HORSE RUNS A RACE

THE LITTLE WOODEN HORSE slept most soundly among the ten white horses, the kindest creatures in the world. They could not do enough to make him feel at home and comfortable – very different from the rough, ill-mannered pit ponies that had treated him so badly.

In the morning he lay for a long time awaiting the miner's little boy, while the grooms watered and fed the white horses with much singing and laughter. When the miner's boy did not come the little wooden horse got up from his comfortable bed of straw and trundled out into the yard to see what he could see. He was noticed almost directly by a fat housekeeper.

"Hey!" she cried. "Here's the little wooden horse

again! Why, my little fellow, you are out of luck this morning, for your young master had hardly finished his soup last night before his father appeared, all nasty and black from the mine – very angry too! He took the boy straight home again without a word, and here you are left all alone. Well, well, well!"

The little wooden horse was most distressed to hear what had happened. He was just about to trundle out of the yard and make his way home after the miner's little boy when a footman came out into the yard and called to him.

"The King wishes to reward you for the services you rendered to him yesterday," he said.

The little wooden horse followed the footman sadly into the royal Palace, along white corridors where his four wheels whispered on velvet carpets and even the coins inside his little wooden body lay still as mice. Presently he came into the King's room, where too were the Queen and the ten little Princes and Princesses.

"Well, my little fellow, I am glad to see you!" said the King. "I am going to give you two golden sovereigns for your work yesterday, and here is another that you will give to your young master to reward him for having such a clever little wooden horse and for bringing him into my city. Now we are all going into the country to see the races. Will you come with us?"

"Oh, *do* come with us!" begged the little Princes and Princesses at once.

"Oh, *do* come with us!" echoed the youngest Princess, Madeleine, long after the others, so that they laughed at her, all except the little wooden horse, who thought her very sweet indeed.

He put the money that the King had given him into the hole in his neck, and when he found that the races lay on the road to the mine he agreed to come and spend the day with the King and the Queen and the ten little Princes and Princesses before returning to the house of his friend the miner's boy.

So by and by they all set off in the royal coach again, for by now the tenth horse had a new shoe and the coach bowled along merrily. The little wooden horse trotted along behind, listening to the chatter of the ten little Princes and Princesses, who were talking about the races, all except the youngest Princess, Madeleine, who chattered to her marionette doll, and peeped over the side of the coach every now and then to smile at the little wooden horse and make sure he was still there.

The races were very fine and splendid. The little wooden horse had never seen so many beautiful animals gathered together as the gleaming racehorses that pranced up and down the course. The little Princes and Princesses ran about looking at them all, except the youngest Princess, Madeleine, who was not allowed to wander about alone, but sat close to her mother's side and chattered to her marionette doll, whom she had brought with her for company.

The races were run, the Princes and Princesses shouted with excitement, the little wooden horse stamped his wooden legs and rattled his wooden wheels. For the moment he wished he were not a little wooden horse at all, but a real, live satin-coated racehorse that could race in front of the King with a jockey no bigger than a monkey on his back.

As the last race drew near the little Princes and Princesses grew more and more noisy, for this was their race. All, that is to say, except the youngest Princess, Madeleine, who was too young to have a race of her own, and hugged her marionette doll, sitting a little wistfully beside her mother and wondering if she could manage to keep awake this year all the way home. She wondered too if Ivor, who was her favourite brother, would win the race and the award of a Golden Trophy that the King gave to the winner among his children, as well as the ten guineas to the winner among the jockeys who rode for them. She wondered what would happen if one of the twins' jockeys came in ahead of the other, or whether Merlin would win, as he did last year, or Belinda, who wanted to so badly!

Up came the nine jockeys on nine beautiful horses. They paused, prancing, before the King and the Queen and the ten little Princes and Princesses – also the little wooden horse, who was standing by the youngest Princess's, Madeleine's, feet, as quiet and solemn as a little wooden owl.

"I ride for the Princess Belinda!" announced the first jockey, mounted on a superb grey horse, as he passed slowly down to the starting-post with a pink ribbon tied to his sleeve, so that they could watch him all the way.

"I ride for the Prince Ivor!" cried a second jockey, with a scarlet ribbon, on a coal-black horse with a flashing eye.

"I ride for the Princess Helena!" cried a third, on a red horse with a white ribbon.

"And I for the Princess April!" cried a fourth, riding a yellow horse with a white ribbon.

"I ride for the Prince Merlin!" announced the fifth jockey, showing his purple ribbon as he pranced by on a piebald horse.

The sixth and seventh jockeys raised their voices together. "We ride for the Princes Sebastian and Llewellyn!" they called loudly.

They were riding two brown horses, as alike as two peas, bearing the same silver ribbon.

The last two jockeys, on dun- and dove-coloured ponies, with orange and royal blue ribbons, called in turn:

"I ride for the Prince Robin!"

"I ride for the Princess Marigold!"

But the youngest Princess, Madeleine, had no one to ride for her, and she could not help looking a little sad as she sat beside her mother, the Queen, wishing that she too were seven years old, and old enough to hear someone calling out, "I ride for the Princess Madeleine!"

The King was clapping the jockeys and the beautiful horses on their way to the starting-post when he felt a gentle tap on his knee, and there stood the little wooden horse.

"If you please, your Majesty," said the little wooden horse, "may I ride for the Princess Madeleine?"

At this the eyes of the youngest Princess, Madeleine, grew round with wonder and excitement, while the King laughed kindly.

"Well, that is an idea!" he said. "She is not yet seven years old, but then you are only a little wooden horse. But where will you find a jockey?"

The little wooden horse's painted eyes fell on the marionette doll that the youngest Princess, Madeleine, had dropped in her excitement.

The King laughed more than ever, but he allowed the little Princess to prop up her marionette doll upon the back of the little wooden horse, and the pair of them trotted away to the starting-post.

"Ha! Ha! Ha! Look at the little wooden horse coming to race for the Princess Madeleine!" whinnied the racehorses, while the jockeys slapped their sides with glee, and rolled about in their saddles, mimicking the marionette doll, who was a very poor rider indeed.

"Get ready!" called the groom at the post, lining up the horses ready to start them off.

The little wooden horse remembered that he bore no coloured ribbon, but the youngest Princess, Madeleine, had tied her rose-pink hair ribbon about the neck of the marionette doll, while there was also his own red saddle and blue stripes. No Princess could wish for better colours!

"*Go!*"

The horses bounded forward with a flashing of

delicate legs, and a rattle of wheels that came from the little wooden horse alone. With his wooden head eagerly forward, his wooden ears pricked, he racketed over the ground side by side with the horses of the twin Princes and the Princess Helena. A little way ahead Prince Ivor's black horse ran like a streak of lightning, while close behind him Prince Merlin's piebald seemed to cut the air with its speed.

The little wooden horse could hear the excited cries and shouts of the ten little Princes and Princesses, watching from beside their father's chair.

"Go on, my black one!" cried the Prince Ivor above all the rest, and below him echoed the tiny voice of the youngest Princess, Madeleine.

"Please win! Please win, my little wooden horse!"

The little wooden horse quickened his pace, just as it seemed that Princess April's yellow horse would pass him. His wheels spun round as he overtook Princess Belinda's grey and galloped side by side with Princess Helena's red horse.

"Now this is a strange thing!" he said to himself. "Here am I, a quiet little horse, quite content to stay at home beside my master, riding in a race for a Princess, and hoping to win a Golden Trophy!"

As he thought this a terrible thing happened, for with a little *click!* out flew one of the nails with which the miner had secured his new wheel, while the wheel itself clattered away under the twinkling legs of the nine galloping horses.

Now the little wooden horse was galloping *cloppetty, cloppetty, cloppetty, clack! cloppetty, cloppetty, cloppetty, clack!* while the marionette doll on his wooden back rolled from side to side, as though at any minute he might roll off altogether.

Behind him the little Princes and Princesses cried out, "Oh! Oh! Look what has happened to Madeleine's little wooden horse! Now he will lose the race!"

This made the little wooden horse more determined than ever to win the race for the youngest Princess, Madeleine, who was silent now; so, telling the marionette doll to sit fast, he bounded forward, *cloppetty, cloppetty, cloppetty, clack! cloppetty, cloppetty, cloppetty, clack!* on his three wheels, till he had overtaken all the horses except Prince Ivor's, Princess Marigold's, and the brown horses belonging to the twin brothers, who were determined to reach the winning-post together.

The little wooden horse heard the youngest Princess cry out again, under the louder voices of her brothers and sisters, "Go on! Go on! Do please win, my little wooden horse!"

"Why, a horse can gallop very well on three wheels after all!" said the little wooden horse, who was making the dust fly as he bounded along.

Bang! Just at that moment another wheel flew off, for the miner's nails were not meant to hold the wheels of a racehorse; and now the little wooden horse was galloping *cloppetty, cloppetty, clack, clack! cloppetty, cloppetty, clack, clack!* and the other horses were coming up fast behind.

The Prince Ivor's black horse turned round to jeer at him.

"Hullo, wooden wheels!" he laughed. "And only two of them at that!" He thought it most amusing to

Bang! Just at that moment another wheel flew off . . .

be racing against a little wooden horse with only two wheels left to gallop on.

The little wooden horse was angry at being mocked by the big black horse, who was leading all the others. In spite of the loss of his two back wheels he galloped along, with the marionette doll swaying and bouncing on the red-painted saddle, and overtook the Princess Marigold's dove-coloured horse – *cloppetty, cloppetty, clack, clack! cloppetty, cloppetty, clack, clack!* – and now only the black horse and the twin Princes' brown ones lay between him and the winning-post.

"Look what has happened to Madeleine's horse! He only has two wheels now!" cried the nine little Princes and Princesses. But the youngest Princess, Madeleine, said nothing at all, except that under her breath she was whispering, "Oh, please do win, my little wooden horse!" Both her little hands were clasped, while her eyes were as round as blue periwinkles.

"Well, a horse goes well enough on two wheels after all!" said the little wooden horse, making a great effort to overtake the horses of the twin Princes, for now the winning-post was getting near.

But just at that minute – *bang!* and a third wheel split clean in half! Certainly the miner had not made them for a little wooden horse to race with.

Now he was galloping *cloppetty, clack, clack, clack! cloppetty, clack, clack, clack!* while the marionette doll dangled over the side of the saddle, ready to fall at any moment.

"Now I *am* finished!" said the little wooden horse, for no wooden horse in the world can gallop his best with three wheels gone and his wooden stand *bump bumping* on the ground at every stride.

So what was his surprise at dropping back to find no horses behind him at all. They had all fallen out of the race, leaving it to him and Prince Ivor's black and the brown horses of the twin Princes, who were gradually losing speed.

Now the ten little Princes and Princesses could hardly contain themselves, particularly the eldest, Prince Ivor, and the twin Princes, Sebastian and Llewellyn. The louder their brother shouted, "Go on, my black beauty!" the louder they yelled out, "Go on, our brown wonders!" till Prince Ivor clapped their heads together in a temper, and for a moment all was confusion. Only the youngest Princess, Madeleine, sat quite still, her round blue eyes fixed on the little wooden horse, who was limping *cloppetty, clack, clack, clack!* behind the rest.

Presently, in spite of the twin Princes' shouts, the two brown horses began to slacken pace and fall farther and farther behind.

Even the black horse was weary; and it was now that the little wooden horse made his last effort. The winning-post drew nearer and nearer – he could see the gay flags flapping in the breeze – and with a bound of his stiff little wooden legs he set his one wheel spinning faster than ever.

On, on – he drew level with the twin brown horses and overtook them. Now they were far behind him, while just ahead the black horse cocked an eye and muttered, "All right, one wheel! I'll show you!" as he galloped faster than ever.

But the little wooden horse was strong, and he was

determined to win the Golden Trophy for the youngest Princess, Madeleine.

He kept doggedly on, *cloppetty, clack, clack, clack!* and little by little he drew level with Prince Ivor's black horse.

The black horse eyed him savagely, for he knew that he himself was tiring and the winning-post was only just ahead.

"Fall back, wooden one!" he ordered, grinding his bit, till the little wooden horse thought again fearfully of the great rocking horse in the little girl's playhouse, away in the forest where he had left Uncle Peder.

But he didn't mean to be afraid of the black horse: he meant to win. Slowly, slowly, he drew ahead. Now the black horse was half a length behind him, breathing hot, angry breath on to his painted back as he angrily tried to get back his place in front of the little wooden horse.

The winning-post was only a few yards ahead, the black horse was nearly beaten, and the little wooden horse was thinking, "Well, after all, if a horse can win a race with only one wheel, that's not so bad!" when a dreadful thing happened. The black horse shot out a wicked hoof and caught the last wheel of the little wooden horse, so that it spun high into the air and then bounded away down the racecourse.

The little wooden horse trundled a few steps farther on, *clack, clack, clack, clack!* and then rolled over and lay still. The marionette doll sprawled beside him on the ground, while the black horse shot past the winning-post to win the race.

The little wooden horse lay still for a long time, while his ears buzzed and stars danced before his painted eyes, and his breath came in great puffs.

"I shall go home," said the little wooden horse. "First I shall give the little boy back his money that lies safely inside my little wooden body, together with the reward that I have for him from the King. And then somehow or other I shall find my way back across the seas to Uncle Peder, for misfortunes come to me in this country. First I lost my eyes, and now I have no wheels. It is better that we should spend our money and starve together than that I should die here alone, with Uncle Peder ill and helpless in the middle of the forest."

As he thought these sad thoughts the little wooden horse became aware of a great shouting going on around him, but this did not disturb him very much. He picked himself up and began to limp, *clack, clack, clack, clack!* back towards the pavilion where the King had sat with the Queen and the ten little Princes and Princesses.

"I will say goodbye," said the little wooden horse. "And then I will go away."

So no one was more surprised than himself when he came to the pavilion and heard all the people shouting, "The little wooden horse has won the race! The little wooden horse has won the race!" And the youngest Princess, Madeleine, rushed up to fling her arms about his wooden neck.

For a great many people had seen how badly the black horse had treated the little wooden horse. The King had seen it, and the Queen, and all the little Princes and Princesses. Even Prince Ivor was standing looking as angry as could be, but his anger was against the black horse, who would not be allowed to take the prize.

So the King handed the Golden Trophy to the youngest Princess, Madeleine, who was so happy that she could not speak for shyness and joy, but ran away from them all to find her marionette doll, who had made a poor jockey, but was none the worse for his fall. The Queen hung a garland round the neck of the little wooden horse, and handed him the prize of ten golden guineas.

"At last I have made my fortune!" said the little wooden horse, sighing with happiness.

The ten little Princes and Princesses begged him to come back with them to the Palace and live with them for ever and ever. But now the little wooden horse was more than ever determined to go back to find Uncle Peder, when he had given the little boy back his money and found someone who would make him four more wooden wheels.

The youngest Princess, Madeleine, cried bitterly when she heard he was going to leave them, till the King, who had heard his story, said, "When you go back to your master, my little wooden horse, you will ask him to make me ten little wooden horses with red saddles and blue stripes, one for each Prince and Princess, and I will pay him five shillings each for them when they are done."

The ten little Princes and Princesses were delighted at the thought of having ten little wooden horses of their own, so they parted happily enough with the little wooden horse, although the youngest Princess, Madeleine, gave him a thousand kisses, and could hardly bear to tear herself away.

11 THE BLACKSMITH AND HIS SON

AFTER SUCH PLEASANT COMPANY the little wooden horse felt lonely limping down the road alone on his way back to the mine.

He could still feel the kisses of the youngest Princess, Madeleine, fluttering like a thousand butterflies about his nose, but for other company he had none, and as night was falling and he was very tired he soon curled up in the shelter of a barn and slept till morning.

The first thing that the little wooden horse heard when he awoke in the morning was the *clink, clink, clink!* of a hammer upon hot metal.

"That sounds to me like a blacksmith's hammer," said the little wooden horse. "And a blacksmith is just the man I want to make me four new, strong little wooden wheels, bound with iron."

So he plodded round the corner of the barn, and

came, sure enough, upon a blacksmith and his son working away in a great smoky forge, where they were shoeing a big red horse.

The blacksmith was rosy-cheeked and handsome, with big, strong hands and a wide, kind smile, but his son was as wizened as a little nut, with a squint in his eye and a crooked, disagreeable mouth.

When they saw the little wooden horse they asked him what he wanted.

"Only four little wooden wheels, bound with iron, to take me on my travels back across the sea," said the little wooden horse very humbly.

The blacksmith shook his head sorrowfully.

"We have no more fuel for our fire," he said. "We have only enough fuel to finish the shoes for the gentleman's horse that you see here, which must be done shortly, for he is going hunting this morning. If the shoes are not ready the gentleman will not pay me, and then we shall have no more money for iron. When they are done my son and I will go into the woods and cut down trees for more fuel, but now we must work until the shoes are ready."

"However," added the blacksmith, seeing how disappointed the little wooden horse appeared, "maybe as your wheels are very small I could heat a little bit of iron in the hot ashes when the shoes are done, but you must wait patiently until I am ready to help you."

The little wooden horse crept into a corner and waited patiently enough while the blacksmith and his son blew sparks from the dying fire and tapped the nails through the shoes of the gentleman's fine red horse. He saw how strong and clever was the blacksmith and how true was his work, while his son drove the nails in crookedly, and hit the horse with the hammer when he would not stand still – behind his father's back.

At last the little wooden horse could bear it no longer.

"That shoe will not hold!" he cried, when the blacksmith's son had driven three crooked nails into the shoe of the red horse.

The blacksmith examined the shoe and rated his son angrily. The son swore and grumbled, cursing at the little wooden horse for giving him away. But the shoe had to come off and be put on again, while valuable moments sped away, and the blacksmith cast anxious glances at the time and at the fire, which was dying away into dusty embers for lack of fuel.

In vain he pumped at the bellows: there was no fire left to burn and another shoe to make. The blacksmith thrust the iron shoe into the ashes, but it would not heat. His brow wrinkled with anxiety, while his son stood sullenly by, looking on.

The blacksmith flung some shavings from the floor on to the fire, and for a few moments the sparks again crackled and blazed, but it was not enough to heat the shoe.

"Wait while I find some wood in the house," said the blacksmith, leaving the forge. "And if there is none there I will pull some straw off the roof."

When he had gone out of the forge the blacksmith's son picked up the little wooden horse and looked at him carefully.

"Well, well, well!" said he, as he heard the coins clinking about inside his little wooden body. "So we carry a fortune inside us, do we?" He rattled the little horse again, and thought what a pleasant sound it was to hear so much money clinking about so close beside him.

Then, he thought, a little wooden horse on a wooden stand was just what he wanted to make the fire blaze and finish the shoes for the gentleman's horse.

"If I take the money out and throw the little wooden horse on the fire," the blacksmith's son said to himself, "my father will think he has got tired of waiting and run away, and the shoes will be finished, while I shall have money to spend for the rest of my life."

The little wooden horse began to tremble violently when he heard what the blacksmith's son was muttering.

"Now here am I, a quiet little horse," he said to himself, "having escaped death by the axe of a little old woman, and by overworking at the hands of a wicked farmer, and by suffocation in the mine, going to be burned in the fire and have all my money taken away! Oh, master! Oh, master! I shall never see Uncle Peder again!"

"So we carry a fortune inside us, do we?"

Just as the blacksmith's son laid him on the edge of the forge and was about to unscrew his head and help himself to the money inside, the little wooden horse screamed out to the red horse, "Oh, help me! Oh, help me, do! I am going to be burned and have all my money stolen!"

The red horse had been growing very restive when he saw what the blacksmith's son was going to do to the little wooden horse, and now he could contain himself no longer. He lashed out with all his might, and knocked the blacksmith's son head over heels across the forge.

The blacksmith's son jumped to his feet and seized his hammer, for he intended to punish the red horse. At the same time he tried to grab the little wooden horse; but they were both too quick for him. The red horse threw up his head and broke his halter. Then he galloped out of the smithy door, closely followed by the little wooden horse.

They galloped away till they were deep in the woods, when they stopped and looked at each other.

The little wooden horse thanked the red horse very

gratefully for saving his life. Then he said, "It seems to me that the good blacksmith is going to get into trouble for no fault of his. When your master goes to fetch you he will find you gone, with only three shoes on, and he won't pay the blacksmith a penny."

"That is true," said the red horse. "Then I will go back directly, for the blacksmith is as kind and pleasant as any man I have met."

"But the fire will be out now," the little wooden horse objected. "And there is no more fuel. The blacksmith will be beating his boy, and the smithy will be empty. We had much better get some more wood for the next fire."

So without delay they set to work gathering branches and boughs, which they carried on their backs, till they could carry no more, and nothing could be seen of the little wooden horse but his straight little legs walking along under a great pile of wood.

They went back to the forge, where the poor blacksmith, having beaten his son, stood beside his empty fire and sighed with despair.

It did not take long to get a new fire going, and while the blacksmith heated the iron the little wooden horse worked at the bellows with all his strength, while the red horse stood as still as a rock to be shod. The last shoe was barely on when his master appeared, in a very good temper at finding his red horse all ready and waiting for him. He paid the blacksmith double what he asked, and galloped away to his hunting.

When they had disappeared the blacksmith made four wooden wheels for the little wooden horse, bound strongly with iron and fastened on with four strong new nails.

"That should last for a while, my little wooden horse," said the blacksmith, who would not take a penny for the wheels, he was so grateful for the fact that the little wooden horse had brought him wood in the nick of time.

12 THE LITTLE WOODEN HORSE AT THE CIRCUS

WITH FOUR NEW WOODEN WHEELS, bound with iron, the little wooden horse rolled along merrily. He expected to be at the home of the miner's little boy by nightfall. The next day he intended to say goodbye and find his way to the coast, whence he hoped some ship would carry him back over the sea to Uncle Peder. Before long he came to a travelling fair – roundabouts, swingboats, tents, and coconut shies – a very gay scene that stretched right across the road. The roaring of tigers and lions, the whistling of boys, and the barking of dogs made the whole place lively enough, and the little wooden horse was rather afraid to pass through the middle of it on his way to the mine.

He thought he would make his way round the edge, in the shelter of the tents.

So he left the road and began to creep around the outside of the fair as softly as his four new wooden wheels would carry him.

By and by he found his way blocked by what appeared to be a thick grey rope that swung and dangled in the air from high above his head. When he tried to pass it by the rope moved too, fumbling and knocking against his head till he could not think what it could be.

"Can it be a snake?" thought the little wooden horse.

Then a terrible thing happened! For all of a sudden the rope curled itself about his wooden body in a tight grey knot and began to lift him into the air! Higher and higher it lifted him – up, up, up! towards the roof of a tent.

"What can this be?" thought the little wooden horse in terror, as he saw the earth getting farther and farther below his new wooden wheels. He could only think of the day when the crane had lifted him up, up, up! from the port, over to the ship, and had dropped him in the hold next to the elephant.

Now the little wooden horse had the strangest surprise – for exactly the same thing happened again! The grey rope began to lower him down, down, down! till it dropped him gently on the straw, and there he was looking up into the kindly face and swaying trunk of his friend the elephant, inside a dark little circus tent no larger than the hold of the ship itself.

"I do believe," said the elephant, "that it is my little friend the wooden horse!"

"And I do believe," said the little wooden horse, "that it is my friend the elephant!"

"*Well!*" both said together, as they told each other how delighted they were with this unexpected meeting.

The elephant was travelling with the circus attached to the fair. He was very interested in the adventures of the little wooden horse, and begged him not to go on his journey immediately.

"Perhaps we shall never meet again," he said sadly. "And when you are gone back over the seas you will forget about me."

The elephant seemed so unhappy that the little

wooden horse agreed to spend a night and a day with him. Besides, he very much wanted to see what part the elephant played in the circus, and how fine he looked dressed up in his scarlet and gold trappings.

When the evening came and the elephant was led out to perform in the circus ring the little wooden horse followed closely at his heels to see what was to be seen.

The elephant was very clever. He stood on his head and performed all kinds of tricks with his trunk and his legs, for which the people threw him buns and clapped him loudly.

The little wooden horse could not clap very well, so he rattled his four new wooden wheels, so loudly that the circus master turned round and saw him.

"Why, what are you doing here, my little wooden horse?" asked the circus master, with an indignant look, for he did not like to have little wooden horses breaking into his circus.

The little wooden horse explained that he had come to see his friend the elephant, but because the circus master still looked rather angry he added that he too could do a lot of tricks.

"For a horse that can win a Golden Trophy on only one wheel must be of some use to a circus," he said to himself.

"Can you stand on your head?" the circus master asked.

"Oh, yes!" replied the little wooden horse, who thought that to a horse who could find his way out of a mine alone standing on his head was nothing.

"Can you gallop backwards?" asked the circus master.

"Why, certainly!" replied the little wooden horse, telling himself that to a horse who had pulled the King's coach three times round the city galloping backwards was very simple.

"Can you walk a tightrope?" asked the circus master.

"Of course!" replied the little wooden horse, who was quite certain by now that he could do anything.

"Then come this way," said the circus master.

Stretched across the roof of the circus tent, high

above the ring, was a tightrope, and it was across this rope that the little wooden horse was expected to walk.

"If you do it well you shall have a silver coin," the circus master promised him, as he helped him up the platform to the tightrope.

Then, while the little wooden horse waited, trembling, to begin, the circus master addressed all the people below.

"Here is the one and only performance of the little wooden horse crossing the tightrope. Keep your places, ladies and gentlemen, please, and watch this miraculous spectacle!"

Far below the little wooden horse saw his friend the elephant gazing upwards with a wondering expression on his kind face. His heart went *pit-a-pat! pit-a-pat!* inside his little wooden body as he thought of what he was going to do.

"Here am I, a quiet little horse who only wants to return home and stay for ever by his master's side," he said, "risking my life on a rope far above the heads of everyone in the world, from where at any moment I may be dashed to death!"

. . . the little wooden horse waited, trembling . . .

But the circus master was cracking his whip, and he had to start out on his dangerous journey across the rope.

The little wooden horse trundled slowly forward, and nobody could tell how his heart was beating inside his little wooden body. Even the coins lay still, and his new wooden wheels made no sound.

Below the people held their breath as he trundled slowly across to the other side, and then there was a burst of applause as silver and copper coins were thrown into the circus ring "for the little wooden horse".

The circus master picked them up and gave them to the little wooden horse with a smile. He gave him, too, the silver coin that he had promised him before, and asked him to stay on and work with the circus: he should have another silver coin for every time that he crossed the rope.

The little wooden horse thought this over very carefully.

"If I stay I shall certainly have a fortune to take to Uncle Peder," he said; "and I am quite close to the mine.

I will stay here for a few days, and then I will go on and give the miner's boy back his money, and make my way to the coast and to Uncle Peder."

So he stayed with the circus, sleeping with the elephant and walking every day across the tightrope till he could do it with his eyes shut. Every day the people threw him money and the circus master gave him a silver coin, till his little wooden body was almost bursting with riches.

Now that he had so much money the little wooden horse found that he had to be very careful indeed upon the tightrope, for the weight of his riches upset his balance. He was a happy little wooden horse.

One evening he had decided it should be his last performance at the circus.

He really had as much money as he knew what to do with: he and Uncle Peder would live in comfort for ever. He doubted if he could put more than five more coins in the hole in his neck, and his little heart was bursting with happiness at the thought of the wealth he was going to bring Uncle Peder.

He climbed the ladder for the last time, and set out bravely and carefully across the rope.

The little wooden horse was halfway across the tightrope, and the people below were holding their breath, when suddenly a clear and well-known little voice called out, "It is! It is! It is my little wooden horse!"

There, sitting in the circus below, was the miner's little boy, whom his father had brought to the fair on his birthday for a treat.

The little wooden horse was so startled he lost his balance. First he swayed to the right side, then to the left, then the weight of his money toppled him over altogether, and he fell into the ring below.

The elephant reached out his trunk and caught him almost in time, but not quite, for one of his little wooden legs was broken. The miner's little boy ran into the ring and picked him up, just as the little wooden horse struggled bravely to his feet.

"Father will mend you! Father will mend you!" said the miner's boy over and over again.

Fortunately, having only wooden legs, the little

wooden horse was not in pain. He decided to go straight home with the miner's little boy and his father, so he limped to the circus master and said goodbye, and to the elephant, with whom he was sorry to part, because they had been good friends.

The circus master paid him double, and asked him to come back to the circus when his leg was healed. "And if you cannot," he told the little wooden horse, "tell your master to make me another little horse as like you as can be, and I will pay him five shillings for such a splendid one as yourself."

Before they set out for home the little wooden horse insisted on giving back to the miner's boy the silver crowns that he had kept for him, and also the King's reward of a golden sovereign. Then, because he was too proud to be carried by the miner or his son, he took to the road behind them, and plodded stolidly down the long, dark road towards the mine.

13 IN THE NURSERY

THE LITTLE WOODEN HORSE was so tired he trundled along in a kind of dream. He was almost too sleepy to notice the kind welcome that was given him by the miner's wife and the baby sister: all he wanted was a corner in which to sleep and rest his broken leg, which had fallen right out of the socket into which Uncle Peder had hammered it so carefully long weeks ago.

By the morning he felt better, and trundled out of the kitchen before anyone was astir to have a long drink at the trough outside the cottage.

"How light and lively I feel this morning!" said the little wooden horse, giving a skip on his three legs that would not have disgraced a lamb. "It seems a horse can do very well on three legs after all."

But he noticed suddenly that no *chink, chink!*

sounded inside his little wooden body when he jumped into the air.

"That is funny," said the little wooden horse, jumping again.

He felt strangely light and empty, while not the faintest tinkle of a coin was to be heard. The little wooden horse began to get anxious. He shook himself, and jerked himself, and galloped in a ring, and stamped his three legs, and even turned head over heels: he felt as light and as empty as air!

At last he took off his head and learned the sad truth: there was not a penny left inside his little wooden body!

The little wooden horse grew quite cold with misery and despair. He tried to think when he had had his money last, and remembered how the coins had clinked when he limped home after the miner's boy and his father. Then he remembered how sleepy he had felt on the way home, and how he had had a funny dream of getting lighter and lighter and lighter all the way.

Suddenly he had an idea. He picked up a pebble

about the size of a penny and dropped it into the hole in his neck. It was just as he had feared. It fell straight out through the hole where his wooden leg had been. *That* was what had happened to his money!

The little wooden horse did not waste a moment, but galloped back up the long road towards the circus. His bright, painted eyes searched everywhere for a glimpse of gold or silver coins, for pennies lying in the dust or shillings in the gutter. He could see nothing.

Money does not lie long on the highway, and already a great many people had passed on the road that morning, to market, to the fields, and to the city. Many people had thought themselves lucky, and gone home richer than they set out.

The little wooden horse found a sovereign at last hidden in the dust under a dock leaf, while some way farther on he discovered a penny. He kept the coins firmly clenched between his little wooden teeth, for he could not trust them again to the treacherous hole in his body.

"I suppose I am a lucky horse to find even so little

of my fortune," said the little wooden horse. But when he thought of the gold and the silver and the riches that he had been going to take home to Uncle Peder the tears came into his painted eyes, and he sobbed as though his wooden heart would break.

"I can do two things now," said the little wooden horse, as he wended his way sadly enough towards the miner's house. "I can get a new leg, for I have, at any rate, a sovereign to pay for it, and I can go back to the circus and earn some more money, or I can go back across the sea to Uncle Peder, and when he has finished making the wooden horses I shall ask him for the little rich girl, the ten little Princes and Princesses, and the circus master we can maybe starve together."

When he had thought all this over the little wooden horse decided not to go back to the circus, for he felt he would never care to walk the tightrope again.

"I will go back to Uncle Peder," said he. "And what will happen will happen."

When he returned to the miner's cottage he said no word about his lost fortune, but he told the little boy that the time had come for him to go home to his real master across the sea.

The miner's boy was very sad to say goodbye to his friend so soon after finding him again, but the miner said, "When you find your master again, little wooden horse, tell him to make another little horse, as fine and as strong as yourself, and I will pay him five shillings out of my wages for such a one for my son."

The miner, his wife, the miner's boy, and the baby sister all came to the door to see the little wooden horse away on his journey to the sea. He would not even stay for the new leg that the miner promised him – not he!

"A horse does very well on three legs," said the little wooden horse.

But before he had gone fifteen miles or so he found out that after all four legs are better than three.

"How tired I am!" thought the little wooden horse, quite surprised to find that a fourth leg could be so important.

When he had trundled twenty miles it became quite clear that he would never reach the coast unless he bought a new leg. His progress became slower and slower, and although his four new wooden wheels spun bravely, his three legs ached so badly they would scarcely hold him up.

When he came to the next village the little wooden horse looked about for someone to help him, and his eye fell on a kind, white-haired old man standing in the doorway of his own toy shop.

"Oh, please, sir," said the little wooden horse, "can you, for a few shillings, make me a new wooden leg?"

"Why, of course, my dear!" replied the kind old shopkeeper. "You have only to come inside and wait while I find a nice little piece of wood."

The little wooden horse was glad enough to go into the shop and rest while the kind old shopkeeper searched about for a stick that would make a good, strong leg.

"And where have you come from, my dear?" he asked.

The little wooden horse told his story while the shopkeeper fitted the new leg into the empty socket. The old man was very interested.

"Now if you ask your master, when you go home, to make me a dozen such strong little horses as yourself," he said, "I will willingly pay him five shillings each for them, for I know I could sell them here in my shop easier than winking."

Sure enough, no sooner had he finished mending the little wooden horse than a gentleman came into the shop.

He was a tall, good-looking man, but he had such a worried expression upon his face that it made the little wooden horse's heart ache to look at him. He wandered all round the toy shop while the good old shopkeeper hammered away at the leg of the little wooden horse, picking up toy after toy, only to lay it down again as if he had no use for it at all.

At last his eye fell on the little wooden horse, whose leg by now was nearly finished.

"Why, what is that?" he asked suddenly. "Now that is a toy I have never seen before!"

"Why, it is a toy that has long been out of fashion," the shopkeeper explained. "I do not think they are made in this country any more. And more is the pity,

I say, for when I was a boy not a child would run out on the pavement without his wooden horse."

So saying the kind old man gave a final tap to the little wooden horse's new leg and set him down on the floor.

"I'll buy that little wooden horse," said the gentleman at once. "For there isn't another toy in your shop that I haven't bought for my children at some time or another, and they are tired of them all. Nothing will keep them quiet except a new toy, and, so far as I can see, there is simply nothing new to be had."

"I am very sorry indeed, sir, but this little wooden horse is not mine to sell," explained the good old shopkeeper in some distress. But now the little wooden horse himself piped up and told his story, to which the gentleman and the shopkeeper listened with great attention and interest.

When he had heard of the lost fortune the gentleman said, "Well, look here, my little wooden horse, how would you like to earn some more money before you go home? If you will come back with me for a week and play with my children I will pay you three silver coins, and I can promise that you will be free after that, for my children get tired of all their toys in a few days; so you will be able to go on your travels as before."

The little wooden horse was very pleased with the idea of earning three silver coins. But before he left the shop with the gentleman he asked the shopkeeper how much he owed him for his new wooden leg.

"Not a penny!" said the kind old shopkeeper. "What is a little piece of wood after all? But don't forget to ask your master to send me a dozen little horses like yourself when you get home, and I will pay him five shillings for every one of them."

When he had thanked the old man over and over again the little wooden horse left the shop and trundled down the street behind the gentleman who had bought him for a week.

Presently they came to a house so full of noise that no one would have believed that all the doors and windows were shut. Children were shouting, crying, screaming, tins were clattering, drums banging, dogs barking.

The gentleman who had bought the little wooden horse opened the door and went in, with the little wooden horse trundling behind him.

No sooner were they in the hall than five or six children hurled themselves down the stairs, arriving at the bottom in a shrieking, kicking mass that gradually found its legs and clustered round the father.

"What have you brought us, Father?" shouted the three little boys and two little girls who had emerged from the tangle.

"I have brought you a new toy," said their father gravely. "You must take it up into the nursery and be quiet."

The five children fell upon the little wooden horse with shrieks of delight, all trying to pick him up at the same time. The little boys pushed their sisters; the little girls slapped their brothers and trod on their hands as they tumbled on the ground. The little wooden horse was seized by his head, his legs, his wheels, his tail, and each of his four legs in turn. It was fortunate for him that all his joints were sound again, or he would have come to pieces in their hands.

"How different they are from the ten little Princes and Princesses!" thought the little wooden horse as he was snatched from hand to hand. He remembered how politely the little brothers had looked after their royal sisters, how unselfishly the little Princesses had given in to the Princes.

Presently the eldest boy, Michael, snatched the little wooden horse out of the hands of his sister Angeline, and with a howl of triumph bounded up the stairs towards the nursery.

Angeline, who had just failed to kick his shins, followed him, with Lavender, Roderick, and Benjamin shouting in the rear. Their father escaped to his own room with a sigh of relief and shut the door.

Michael arrived in the nursery well ahead of his brothers and sisters. He threw the little wooden horse behind the window curtain and swaggered about to wait till they arrived.

From a chink in the curtains the little wooden horse could look out into the nursery. Only once before had he seen so many toys together. That was in the playhouse belonging to the little girl, away in the forest where he had left Uncle Peder. But those toys had been gay and bright, well looked after, and tidily arranged on their shelves. These were lying higgledy-piggledy all over the room, and all were broken, cracked, or scratched – a pitiful collection!

The little wooden horse turned his painted eyes away from them in shame, just as the four other children burst into the room.

"What have you done with Father's present, Michael?" they all yelled.

Michael would not tell them, so they all began to fight, and presently the youngest little girl, Lavender, discovered the little wooden horse behind the window curtain, so they fought *her* for a change. When it was all over the little wooden horse felt as bruised and as battered as when the little old woman had flung him high over her roof and he had landed *plump!* in her cabbage bed.

After that they played with him awhile, galloping him round and round the nursery till his four wooden wheels rattled again; and by bedtime he was so dizzy that he did not mind whether he slept on a bed of straw or on the hard floor in the corner of the nursery, where they left him.

The next day the children found that his head came off, and that there were two coins in his inside. This surprised them very much, but for all their naughtiness they were honest children, so they left the coins alone. Only they filled him up with marbles, which were very heavy and uncomfortable, rattling about in his inside like stones, till for the first time in his life the little wooden horse had a stomach-ache.

This went on for days: the little wooden horse was played with and quarrelled over and galloped round and round the nursery, along the corridors, even up and down the stairs, but, strange to relate, the children did not get tired of him. They never went to their father now demanding new toys: they wanted nothing better than the little wooden horse.

He himself was feeling battered and worn. He longed for the end of the week, so that he might go on his journey to join Uncle Peder. Even the dishonest Farmer Max had not treated him as these

. . . the children did not get tired of him.

children did: his paint was chipped all over his body, his tail thin with being tugged, his wheels splintering already from galloping round the nursery floor.

"Only two days – only one day more," he said to himself as the end of the week drew near. "Then I shall take my payment and go."

The children had no idea that they were to lose their favourite toy so soon, for their father had told them nothing. He had been sure that they would get tired of the little wooden horse long before the week came to an end.

On the very last day of all the youngest child, Benjamin, managed to steal the little wooden horse when the rest were not looking, and ran with him into the garden. It was the first time he had been able to play with him alone, and Benjamin was delighted.

He took him down to the stream and gave him a drink. Then he put him in the water to see if he would swim.

"Poor little wooden horse!" said Benjamin when the little wooden horse sank to the bottom immediately.

"Of course you can't swim when you are full of my brothers' heavy marbles."

He took the little wooden horse out of the stream and emptied all the marbles into his own pockets, which relieved the little wooden horse considerably, for the marbles had been almost more than he could bear. Benjamin then put back the two coins and screwed on his head, for he was an honest little boy.

He was a careless little boy too, and he had not screwed the little wooden horse's head back firmly into its socket.

Now the little wooden horse swam bravely, while Benjamin ran up and down the bank shouting for joy, when all of a sudden a big piece of wood floating down the stream charged the little wooden horse and knocked his head off before he could say a word.

Benjamin screamed and plunged into the stream. He seized the little wooden horse's body and pulled him out of the water just as he was beginning to drown, with the water rushing into the hole in his neck – *glug-glug-glug!* But his wooden head, with its painted, staring eyes went rushing away down the stream out of sight.

Benjamin ran down the bank, but it was too late: there was nothing he could do but sit on the bank and sob, clasping the little wooden horse with both hands as the water dripped off them both in round, wet, melancholy tears.

It was here that Benjamin's brothers discovered him when they came to punish him for stealing their wooden horse; and when they had finished buffeting and punching him, and his sisters had joined in with slaps and pinches, they suddenly discovered the dreadful thing that had happened to the little wooden horse's head, so they began all over again, till some of them had fallen in the stream, and Benjamin was black and blue.

For the rest of the day nobody would speak to him, and when the evening came the eldest boy, Michael, put the little wooden horse under his own bed and dared anybody to take him away.

The little wooden horse could not sleep for sorrow and the thought of his lost head. The week was over, and the next day he would start on his travels again. But where was a horse without a head?

At last he became so miserable he decided he could not bear to wait any longer. For one thing the children might prevent him from going, and for another he was determined to have one more look for his wooden head by the banks of the stream before he set out on his journey home.

Very quietly he crept out from beneath Michael's bed and began to trundle across the floor. He had just reached the door when one of his wheels gave a terrible squeak, and Michael sat up in bed.

"What's that?" he said. "Halt! Who goes there?"

"What is it?" asked Roderick sleepily, waking up too.

"I was dreaming of soldiers. I thought I was a sentry," said Michael, burying his head in the pillow, and the little wooden horse slipped out of the door unseen.

All thoughts of the money he was to have earned had gone out of his head. He only wanted to leave the house and escape from those dreadful children. His little heart nearly jumped out of the hole in his neck when, as he was passing a door that was slightly ajar, another voice called out sternly, "Who goes there?"

It was the children's father this time, sitting up

in bed in his pyjamas, blinking at the little wooden horse, who, after hesitating for a little, pushed open the door and went inside.

"If you please, sir," he said very humbly, "the week you mentioned is over, and I am battered and bruised and have lost my head. If you please, I want to go home now, and end my days with my master, who is across the sea."

"But you haven't been paid yet!" said the children's father, jumping out of bed and fetching from his dressing table three silver coins, which he slipped down the neck of the little wooden horse. "I had hoped," he added, "that you would stay another week, for I have never seen the children happy so long with one toy, and now they will come clamouring to me again. I am very sorry indeed that they have been so rough with you and battered your paint and lost your head, but if I give you three more silver coins and ask the old shopkeeper to make you a new head and give you a new coat of paint, will you stay another week and play with my children?"

But the little wooden horse could not consider

this, for he had never been so battered in his life, and the thought of another week of the same treatment was more than he could endure.

"If you please, sir, I would rather go home," he said.

The children's father did not attempt to prevent him.

"Well," he said, "I dare say you are right. All I ask is that when you return to your master you ask him to make me five little wooden horses like yourself, one for each of my children, and I will willingly pay him five shillings for every one of them."

Then he said goodbye very kindly to the little wooden horse, who trundled away down the stairs out into the moonlight.

14 THE SWIM TO THE SEA

THE LITTLE WOODEN HORSE trundled down the garden path, and it was fortunate that he had no painted eyes with which to see his shadow in the moonlight, for it was as ridiculous a shadow as one could hope to see – just a little round body with no head and four straight drumsticks of legs on chipped wooden wheels.

When he came to the stream the little wooden horse jumped into the water, although the moon had made it icy cold, and began to swim down with the current, feeling the banks on either side, in case his head had caught up in the rushes. It would be terrible to pass it by!

But the water carried him along rapidly, just as it had carried his head many hours before. There were no rushes to hinder him, just green banks and the swiftly flowing water lapping like a cold necklace round the body of the little wooden horse.

He had to keep his neck well above water, for if any came in his wooden body would fill, and he would be drowned. So he did his best not to be taken by surprise by any rough water, or thrust under the surface by overhanging branches, and swam bravely on.

He nearly came to a terrible end some way down the stream, when he was already several miles below the children's home. For some while he had heard a roaring and splashing of water ahead of him, and had wondered what it was. As the noise drew nearer the stream became swifter and swifter, carrying him along like a tiny round cork on four wheels.

Suddenly he realized that he was coming to the weir above the mill, and if he ever swam into that tangled jungle of waters he would never keep the waves out of the hole in his neck, and he would be drowned.

The little wooden horse swam to the bank with all his might, and managed to land just above the weir, trembling all over with terror.

When he thought of his poor little head being

hurled down into the same mass of waters so short a time before the little wooden horse began to sob with despair.

"I shall never, never find my wooden head," he wept. "Why didn't I stay behind as the gentleman suggested, and get a new head made by the kind old shopkeeper?"

Then he remembered how Uncle Peder had made the old head, and no one could make such heads as he.

"Perhaps he would not recognize me in a new head," the little wooden horse said to console himself. "I will go back to him without my head, and he will make me a new one."

So he trundled down the bank of the stream past the weir, where the water roared past the mill, and on to calmer waters. Then he plunged into the stream again and swam on, with the moon fading in the sky and a grey dawn breaking in the east.

By the time the sun had risen the little wooden horse was so exhausted it was all he could do to keep the hole in his neck out of the water. Now and then, in fact, a cold little trickle entered in spite of his care, and shivered its way down into his inside among the coins. When that happened he swam harder than ever, but he was very, very tired.

Only one thing kept him from climbing out on the bank to rest among the reeds, and that was the far-off smell of the sea, which had been becoming more and more distinct ever since the sun rose. Somewhere, at the end of the stream, which had now widened into a broad river, miles away, perhaps, there was a seashore bounding the sea, and beyond the sea was Uncle Peder!

The sun rose higher and higher; far beyond, on the horizon, gleamed a silver line – the waves! But the little wooden horse could not see it. He no longer had any painted eyes to see with, and anyway he was too exhausted to notice anything at all.

Now the noise of the waves could be heard bringing in the morning tide, the crying of gulls, the screams of the terns; but the little wooden horse's neck was sinking lower in the water, as more and more frequently little trickles of cold water ran down into the hole and into his inside.

"I shall drown," thought the little wooden horse,

who was no longer swimming: he let the water carry him. He no longer had the strength to drag himself out of the water on to the bank. Nothing mattered any more: he was going to die.

Now the river flowed faster and faster, for it was about to meet the sea. As it flowed it filled the hole in the neck of the little wooden horse, so that he sank deeper and deeper into the water: but he was not yet drowned. The river flowed so fast that it carried him along in spite of himself, and now the roar of the waves on the beach was louder than the roar of the river. The little wooden horse did not hear either of them: he was so nearly drowned.

Down on the seashore a donkey man and his little wife had come to give their donkeys a drink where the fresh river water ran into the sea.

Just now they paused to examine a very curious thing that the donkey man's dog had found lying on the beach.

"It came out of the sea," said the donkey man.

"It came out of the river," said the donkey man's wife.

Just now they paused to examine a very curious thing . . .

"Somebody left it on the shore," said the donkey man.

The dog wagged his tail, looked wise, and said nothing.

"It's a head," said the donkey man's wife.

"It's a boat, or part of one," said the donkey man.

"It's a head, I tell you, and there is the body that belongs to it!" screamed the donkey man's wife, as the river plunged under the gravel bank that divided it from the sea and threw up the body of the little wooden horse at their feet.

The donkey man picked up the body and carefully emptied it of all the river water that was inside. When the coins came rolling out he opened his eyes wide with astonishment, but he was an honest man, and when he had counted them he put them back again.

"That is his own business, I suppose," said the donkey man, while his wife nodded wisely.

Then they put the little wooden horse's head back on to his body, and were as pleased as children to see how well both fitted.

The little wooden horse was even more delighted

than they, but as yet he felt too weak to do more than blink his painted eyes and flap his wooden ears once or twice backwards and forwards. Then he heaved a deep sigh of satisfaction and looked around him, hardly believing his eyes when he saw that at last he really had come to the sea.

15 BLACK JAKEY

THE DONKEY MAN and his wife led the little wooden horse back to the tiny stable on the seashore where they kept their donkeys.

Then when he had had a good meal and was warm and dry again he felt well enough to thank them both gratefully for saving his life and his head, after which he told them his story, and asked if there were any boats calling soon that would take him across the sea to Uncle Peder.

The donkey man said it was unlikely that any boats would call for a week or so, but meanwhile how would he like to earn a little money by working for the donkey man, giving rides on the shore to the children who came down to the sea for their holidays? The donkeys were old and lazy, the donkey man said. A little wooden horse would be something new.

The little wooden horse was quite pleased with this idea. The passage across the sea would cost him some of his silver coins, he knew, but because the donkey man had saved his life the little wooden horse offered to help him for nothing. The donkey man and his wife would not hear of this, so it was decided that the little wooden horse should keep half of everything he earned.

Most of the children on the shore were tired of the donkeys, but when they saw the little wooden horse they came in crowds. He was kept busy all day long, but the sands were firm and dry. It was no hardship to him to trundle up and down carrying laughing children on his back; they did not quarrel over him as the children had done in the house he ran away from.

The donkeys were very friendly to him. He was more popular than they, so they had very little work to do, which pleased them very well. On the other hand, the little wooden horse earned a great many pennies, and in the evening the donkey man gave him a whole silver coin, which was as much as he had earned from the circus master. The little wooden horse no longer mourned over his lost fortune. "In a few days I shall have a new one," he said.

The donkeys' master and his wife were very good to him. They fed him well, and would not allow him to work too hard. Every morning he trotted along to the end of the shore to see if a boat were coming in that day, but there was never one to be seen, and he had to come back disappointed.

"Never mind, one will come tomorrow," said the little wooden horse.

Meanwhile he was very happy indeed, his only sorrow being that he could not repay the donkey man and his wife for all they had done for him.

"Pay us!" they laughed, throwing up their hands. "What should we want payment for? As if you haven't earned more money for us this summer than we have gained for many a year!"

There was another donkey man on the beach, as mean and bad-tempered as the first was jolly and kind. His donkeys were thin and unkempt, he charged too much for donkey rides, and nobody went near him. He hated the little wooden horse's friends after this, and one day he packed up and left the shore for another seaside place. Everyone was very glad to see him take himself and his bad-tempered beasts away.

Two nights after Black Jakey, as he was called, had left the shore the little wooden horse, who slept with the donkeys, was awakened by a stealthy step outside the shed.

He pricked up his wooden ears and listened. A moment later Black Jakey peeped round the door of the stable.

"Now that is a funny thing!" said the little wooden horse. "Whatever can Black Jakey be doing here?"

He soon guessed what Black Jakey was after when he saw him creep into the stable and unfasten the halter of the best and the sleekest of the donkeys.

"Now whatever shall I do?" said the little wooden horse to himself. "Shall I go and tell the donkey man that Black Jakey is stealing his donkeys, or shall I rouse the dog that sleeps on the bed of the donkey man's wife?"

Then he saw that Black Jakey was carrying an

ugly-looking cudgel. Anybody who tried to stop him now would have a bad time.

"I must do it myself," said the little wooden horse.

He was too prudent to attack Black Jakey. He decided to follow him.

The donkey man's donkeys were sleek and fat. They were also greedy. Caliban was the greediest of them all, and when Black Jakey offered him sugar and carrots he followed him out of the stable willingly enough, hoping for more. Black Jakey gave him more, too, until they were out of sight of the donkey man's stable, when he broke into a jog-trot, pulling the donkey after him by the rope on his halter.

Behind them, with his wooden wheels rolling as quietly as possible, came the little wooden horse.

Now and then Black Jakey stopped to listen, as if he suspected that someone was following him. When he did this the little wooden horse stopped too, crouching in the shadows so that he should not be seen.

Once the donkey himself heard the little wooden

horse following. He looked round and brayed a welcome.

Black Jakey immediately stuffed his mouth with carrots, so that he could not bray any more, while the little wooden horse stayed as still as a mouse in the shadow of the bushes they were passing.

They left the sea and wended their way inland, where the country lay quiet and still, unlapped by the waves. The little wooden horse did not like leaving the sea behind: it seemed like turning his back on Uncle Peder, and he had the crazy idea that a boat might come in while he was away; but he owed this duty to the donkey man, and was determined to carry it out.

When they had walked a long way in the dark they heard some distance ahead of them the long, mournful bray of another donkey, and Caliban, who had begun to lag, quickened his pace and answered it. This time Black Jakey let him bray his heart out without trying to stop him. A few moments later they came upon a little tent pitched beside a furze bush on the heath. Behind the tent three starved-looking donkeys were tethered.

When Black Jakey arrived at his tiny camp the three donkeys laid their ears back and immediately attacked Caliban with their hoofs. Black Jakey hit them all round, and tied Caliban up out of their reach, with a piece of cord between his front legs for greater safety. Then with a weary grunt he crawled into his tiny tent to sleep till morning. His own three donkeys also settled down to sleep, while Caliban, a little lonely in his new surroundings, and finding no more carrots or sugar, began to tramp foolishly round the stake to which he was tied and shake his forefeet in perplexity.

When all was quiet the little wooden horse, who had been hovering in the shadows, crept silently through the furze till he came to Caliban's side. He had no liking for the donkey, who was greedy and lazy, but he did not mean to allow Black Jakey to steal him from the donkey man. Caliban, he saw, had no idea he had been stolen: he would go anywhere for food.

When Caliban saw the little wooden horse trundling silently through the furze bushes towards him his eyes nearly popped out in his astonishment.

"So it *was* you behind us all the time!" he exclaimed. "Well, well, well! I would have dropped a carrot for you if I had believed it, for there seem to be plenty about."

"Plenty about!" scoffed the little wooden horse. "You won't sing that song tomorrow! I don't expect you'll ever see a carrot again, so long as you stay with Black Jakey. Not that you are going to stay," he added determinedly. "For I have come to take you home."

As he spoke he was carefully unfastening Caliban's rope from the stake where he was tied.

"Take me home! Whatever next?" blustered the donkey. "I suppose I can stay where I please, can't I? I suppose I can serve whichever master treats me best? And as for the carrots, Black Jakey still has a great bag of them, for I saw them with my own eyes."

"Well, *you* won't see any more of them," said the little wooden horse, holding the end of the rope firmly between his teeth. "Come along, and step quietly."

"I'm not coming!" said Caliban angrily, sticking all his feet obstinately into the ground. "I've been a long walk already tonight, and I'm not going all that way back again just to please you. You go back to my old master if you want to, and leave me alone. I know when I'm well off."

"Ah!" said the little wooden horse. "You won't say that tomorrow. Everyone knows how Black Jakey treats his donkeys. No food, no bedding, no shelter at night! Haven't you seen them on the shore? Haven't you noticed how their ribs poke and stare? How will you enjoy sharing the life of three such bad-tempered brutes as those which kicked at you tonight?"

"That's different," said Caliban. "Black Jakey is good to *me*. He gives me delicate things to eat. Run home, little wooden horse, but before you go be so good as to unfasten the rope between my two front legs, for Black Jakey need not be afraid. I shall not attempt to run away."

"Here, you new animal down there!" one of the other donkeys brayed suddenly. "Stop your muttering and complaining. We can't go to sleep, and if Black Jakey hears you he'll come out and flay the skin off your back, and ours too, and besides that he'll kick you to death in the morning."

In spite of himself Caliban could not help shivering when he heard these fierce words.

"There, you see!" said the little wooden horse, pulling more firmly than ever at Caliban's rope. "What do you think of your new life now? Would your old master flay you alive, or your old friends kick you to death?"

"They didn't mean it," said Caliban, still trembling. And to hide his fear he called out boldly, "All right, you poor knock-kneed sheep! Black Jakey is my friend. If he takes off your skins he will spare mine. And if you raise your hoofs against me Black Jakey will break all your legs."

There was a sudden roar of indignation from the little tent as Black Jakey came lumbering out, his eyes dazed with sleep.

"Can't you let a man sleep, you good-for-nothing brute?" he shouted at Caliban, hurling his heavy cudgel with all his strength at the donkey's head. "I'll take it out of you tomorrow if you don't stop your braying!"

Now Caliban's legs shook until he could hardly

stand upright. The little wooden horse could feel him trembling right down to the shoes on his feet, as he worried at the knots with his little wooden teeth and tried vainly to unfasten the rope that joined Caliban's forelegs.

Black Jakey had tied them too securely, and the little wooden horse had to give it up. He was a little shaken himself, for the cudgel had grazed both their heads and landed in a furze bush a few feet away.

"Very well," he said coldly. "I will go back alone and leave you here."

But now Caliban was far too terrified to stay behind.

"Take me too!" he pleaded. "You were quite right, my little wooden horse. I can't possibly stay in such a terrible place with so wicked a man and such bad-tempered donkeys. I should die in a week. Take me back to my old master, my little wooden horse. Oh, do!"

"How will you walk with that rope around your legs?" asked the little wooden horse severely.

"Oh, I'll limp! I'll hobble! I'll limp a hundred miles

to leave this horrible spot!" said Caliban piteously. "Only take me away directly, my little wooden horse, before Black Jakey comes out to find his cudgel and belabours me with it!"

The little wooden horse began to lead the way carefully through the furze, away from the tent, with Caliban shuffling in the rear. Every other moment they stopped to listen, but all they could hear were the snores of Black Jakey and the deep sighing of the sleeping donkeys tethered behind the tent.

"Oh, what a fool I am!" sighed the donkey Caliban, hobbling and stumbling behind the little wooden horse. "Why did I ever let myself be taken out of my nice warm stable? I shall never get home with my legs tied up so that I can hardly take a step without falling."

Suddenly in the darkness behind them arose a shrill bray.

"Where are you going, stranger donkey? Where has the stranger donkey gone?"

Two more donkey voices joined in the braying chorus.

"Where has the stranger donkey gone?"

The next moment there were grunts, blows, and shouts, as Black Jakey left the tent and laid about him with his second stick.

The little wooden horse pulled the shivering Caliban deep into a furze bush, and made him lie as still as a mouse while they listened to Black Jakey saddling one of the donkeys and following them at a canter.

"More fool you to wake him!" the two donkeys that were left jeered, as the donkey Black Jakey rode grunted and complained at being ridden across the heath at such an hour of the night.

Poor Caliban was so terrified he could not move or breathe. Close beside him the little wooden horse crouched, listening to Black Jakey's threats as he galloped round and round the tiny camp in an ever wider circle.

"I'll thrash him! I'll flay him when I catch him! I'll work him fourteen hours a day! I'll starve him for a week! I'll clip his coat till his own master won't know him!"

"I'll bite him!" the donkey joined in, grunting,

The little wooden horse began to lead the way . . .

as he galloped. "I'll kick him! Between us we'll make his life a burden! That will teach him to keep us awake at night, and take us out galloping all over the moor, spoiling the only bit of peace we get in the day!"

The more they threatened the more Caliban shook, till he might have trotted out and given himself up in sheer terror, but the little wooden horse kept him still and told him not to be afraid. Three times Black Jakey passed so close to their hiding place that it seemed they were bound to be discovered, but at last he gave it up as a bad job, and trotted back to camp, still muttering threats and curses under his breath.

Caliban would have tried to escape at once, but it was a long while before the little wooden horse would let him go. He was afraid Black Jakey might be listening, or the donkeys would hear and tell tales again.

At last they crept out of the bush, stiff, sore, and full of prickles, and began to make their painful way back to the seashore.

Caliban could only hobble so slowly that it was long past sunrise when they limped into the stable, to find the donkey man sitting in the empty stall with his head in his hands, for he had arisen with the lark as usual, and had found both his best donkey and his friend the little wooden horse had disappeared.

When he saw them come in tears of joy ran down his ruddy cheeks, and as he listened to their story he kept interrupting them to kiss one or the other upon the nose.

They both slept far into the day, by which time Black Jakey, afraid of being caught and punished, had taken his tent and donkeys away to a far seashore where nobody would be likely to find them.

16   THE LITTLE WOODEN HORSE
SWIMS THE OCEAN

DAY AFTER DAY PASSED, but no boats came, till at last the little wooden horse grew pale and sad. He worked his best, as ever, but soon the donkey man noticed that his spirits were lacking, while now and then tears stood in his painted eyes and rolled on to the sand.

"Don't cry, my little wooden horse," he begged. "Sooner or later a ship is sure to come, and then you can return to your master over the sea. But meanwhile think of the fortune that you are making and the riches you will be able to take home with you!"

It was true that the little wooden horse had earned a great deal of money. Working for the donkey man on the seashore, he had saved enough to keep himself and Uncle Peder in moderate comfort for a long time to come. But the summer was drawing to an end, soon there would be no more children staying on the shore, the donkey man and his little wife would take their donkeys into the country for the winter, and if no boat came then, what would become of the little wooden horse?

One afternoon the little wooden horse saw a large crowd of people following a tall man down to the shore. The tall man shone all over like a fish in his swimming suit as he entered the water. The people beside him did not go into the water: they gathered round the edge, cheering and waving their hands as the tall, shining man swam out to sea.

Three men got into a boat and rowed beside him: they rowed and rowed till the boat was just a little speck on the water, while the tall and shining man could not be seen at all.

"What a lot of fuss to make about one man swimming out to sea!" said the little wooden horse in surprise, when the people on the shore had finished shouting and waving and had gone home.

"Ah," said Caliban, who had seen it happen before,

"that is not an ordinary swimmer, like those you see in the water every day. He means to swim to the other side of the sea. That is why his body shines like a fish: he is covered with oil, so that he can stay in the water for a long time and not feel the cold. The people whom you saw in the boat will feed him when he gets hungry, and some time he will arrive at the other side."

The little wooden horse's heart bounded with sorrow. Here was a little boat going right across the sea, and he had not so much as asked to be taken too. He had mistaken it for an ordinary fishing boat, going a little way out to sea and coming back in the evening.

"Oh, what a foolish little horse I am!" said he. Then he became very thoughtful, and for the rest of the day and night he said very little, but his mind worked all the time.

In the morning he went to find the donkey man.

"Dear master," he said, "as you know, I have been waiting a very long time for a boat to take me home across the sea, and no boat has come. Now I don't think I can wait any longer. Yesterday a man entered the water and swam out of sight across the sea. I can do that too. I am only a little wooden horse, but I am a strong one, and I have already been many hours in the water without harm. Tomorrow morning, if you will forgive me, I shall try and swim across the ocean."

The donkey man and his wife both shed tears when they heard that the little wooden horse was going to leave them, and in so dangerous a manner, but they did not try to stop him, for they knew how long and patiently he had waited, and how anxious he was to get back to Uncle Peder, who had made him.

When the morning came the donkey man's little wife covered him all over with her best hot dripping, till he was as greasy as a pancake, and gave him a drink of hot soup to set him on his way.

Then, accompanied by Caliban and the other donkeys, all very sad and tearful, the donkey man and his wife went down to the seashore with the little wooden horse and watched him trundle into the water.

All the donkeys brayed, the little wife sobbed, and the donkey man blew his nose loudly. The little wooden horse himself could not suppress a sob as he turned for a farewell toss of his head, which gleamed in the sun like a silver image, the donkey man's wife had so plastered him with dripping.

When the little wooden horse looked round again he was a long way from the shore, and his friends had gone back to their work. He could just see the little brown stable standing on the seashore, and he felt rather lonely when he found himself so far from his friends, with such a long distance ahead of him to swim. He could not see any shore ahead, only sea – green, blue, and silver, immeasurably wide.

The little wooden horse swam on and on till the morning sky turned hot and blue with midday heat. Then, very slowly, the sun began to disappear.

"What can this mean?" said the little wooden horse. "Can it be night already?"

But it was not night. He could still see the sun shining palely above him through a thick haze that seemed to be settling on the sea all about him.

"Whatever can it be?" said the little wooden horse.

Now the sea changed colour as slowly as the sky.

The clear green lights faded out of the waves, which rose and fell in an ominous swell that lifted the little wooden horse high at one moment, only to dash him into black and grey valleys of water the next. He became a little frightened.

He could see no land ahead of him, or behind him or on either side.

"I am right in the middle of the ocean," said the little wooden horse.

Blacker and blacker grew the weather. Great clouds rolled up behind the haze, piled like mountains in the sky. The sea was a terrible colour.

The little wooden horse swam bravely on, trying to imagine that all was sunshine and blue water as before. He shut his painted eyes and pretended that ahead of him lay a golden shore, opening out into a road that led straight to the forest and Uncle Peder. But when he opened his eyes the sky was blacker than ever, while the sea flung him about in a manner that gave him strange and peculiar feelings in his inside.

All of a sudden he was surprised to hear a

familiar sound. That is to say, almost familiar, for the noise that he heard was not quite like the noise that he was accustomed to. It sounded like the whinnying of a great many ponies, and yet not quite ordinary ponies, for the noise was bound up with the whistle of the wind and the roar of the sea, so that it had a new note, and the little wooden horse wondered what on earth it could be.

He was so lonely and so glad to hear anyone else alive in this tremendous waste of sea that he forgot to be cautious, and whinnied back at the top of his little wooden voice. All the coins in his inside rattled as he whinnied, and the gulls overhead flew away screaming with fear. Almost immediately a whole peal of shrill neighs answered him, as swimming over the crest of the next wave came a dozen beautiful little white horses.

The little wooden horse had never seen such beautiful, fairylike creatures. Their manes and tails streamed in the wind like silken banners, their proud little heads tossed and bowed, spray flew from their nostrils. They skimmed over the tops of the waves with such ease that the little wooden horse felt awkward beside them.

These beautiful little creatures swam round and round him, uttering their high, piercing whinnies, whether friendly or indignant it was hard to tell. The little wooden horse felt quite humble, and wondered how he had dared to reply to them.

"What are you, you funny little thing?" one of them cried at last, when the whole herd of them had swum three or four times round the little wooden horse.

"Oh, please, I'm just a little wooden horse, swimming back home to my master over the sea. I'm a quiet little horse, I am; I don't want to disturb anybody. I only want to return to my master's side and stay there quietly for ever and ever."

"A *horse*, did he say?" cried one of the lovely little creatures, tossing its white mane as it reared up on the crest of a wave. "But *we* are horses! How dare you call yourself a horse! Look at you! Are you *like* a horse, I'd like to know? How dare you come and swim in our sea!"

"Uncle Peder told me I was a horse when he

made me," replied the little wooden horse, very humbly. "So a horse I suppose I am. After all, I have two ears –"

"Painted wooden ears!" jeered the sea horses, tossing their lovely heads.

"I have two eyes –"

"Painted round eyes!" laughed the sea horses.

"A mane and tail –"

"Made of black wool!" sang the sea horses, as their own silken manes streamed in the wind.

"Then I have a body –"

"Painted with blue stripes!" jeered the sea horses, curving their graceful bodies to the waves.

"I have four strong wooden legs –"

"Legs!" screamed all the sea horses together. "Whoever heard of a horse with legs? Why, horses have *fins*!"

"And I have four strong wooden wheels," added the little wooden horse desperately.

"Wheels!" the beautiful creatures cried. "What are wheels? What does a horse want but a tail to swim with?"

And as the next wave lifted them high every sea horse reared up against the darkening sky and showed, in place of legs and wheels, their graceful fins and silver tails.

The little wooden horse felt quite abashed.

"Uncle Peder told me a horse had legs and four wooden wheels when he made me," he said. "I suppose he was right after all."

"How dare such a creature call himself a horse!" the sea horses raged in mock anger. "Let's chase him off the sea! Let's get rid of the little monster!"

With a hundred piercing whinnies and squeals of joy the white horses plunged down the next wave after him, their manes flying wildly. Others hurried to join them. Soon the sea was full of the fairylike creatures, all chasing the poor little wooden horse, who had to flee for his life.

"How dare you call yourself a horse!" they shrieked, tossing their heads gaily, delighted with the hunt.

"He's a fox! A sea fox!" cried a new horse, who had just joined it. The rest took up the cry with whinnies of delight.

"A sea fox! A hunt! We'll hunt the sea fox!"

"I'm a horse! I'm a horse!" the little wooden horse cried when he could spare a minute for breath. For Uncle Peder had made him a horse, and a horse he was determined to be. "I may be drowned," said the little wooden horse, "or killed by these cruel creatures, but a horse I shall die."

He was now being chased by at least a thousand of the mischievous, proud little sea horses. Their shrill neighs and whinnies filled the air; they screamed with joy as the little wooden horse fled before them. "After him! After him!" they cried.

The little wooden horse felt his breath going. He had been swimming all day, and who could tell how far yet he must go to reach the shore? His wooden legs ached; he could no longer feel his wheels, and longed to rest a little, floating on the surface of the sea, till his breath returned. But if he stopped for a moment he would be caught by the beautiful, wicked sea horses, and how they meant to punish him for calling himself a horse he did not like to think.

Suddenly a dark shape loomed ahead of him, almost hidden at one moment by the great waves, but at the next the whole of its enormous hulk came into view. A big ship was riding into the storm, right across the path of the little wooden horse.

When he saw the ship the little wooden horse's courage rose again.

"Oh, if only I could hide myself in the wash of that big ship!" he said. "These terrible creatures would never find me then!"

The sea horses neighed still more shrilly when they saw the big ship, and rode the waves even faster than they had done before. The little wooden horse could feel the salt spray from their nostrils stinging his painted back. They had nearly caught him. Then a strange thing happened, for the ship stopped, and a sailor swung himself down the side on a rope ladder. Hanging like a monkey from the rungs, he waited till the exhausted little wooden horse had reached the side of the vessel, when he stooped and snatched him up, right out of the jaws of the sea horses, who reared and battered against the timbers of the ship, neighing their anger and disappointment at being robbed of their prey.

The little wooden horse's heart continued to beat with fright while the sailor climbed the ladder to the deck with him, and below the sea horses neighed and snorted around the boat.

On deck half a dozen sailors crowded about the man who had saved his life, laughing and teasing him.

"So that is what you saw on the water – a child's toy! That's a pretty piece of rubbish to stop the ship for!"

The sailor, who was called Left-handed Peter, smiled a little sheepishly as he put the little wooden horse down on the deck.

"Well, it's a pretty enough toy for all that," he said.

"Well, what are you going to do with it?" the sailors jeered at him. "You haven't any children. Will you take it to your sweetheart?"

Left-handed Peter did not enjoy being teased, and he knew his sweetheart would not thank him for a wooden horse. He meant to buy her a beautiful red shawl at the next port they touched. So he left the

The sea horses neighed . . . They had nearly caught him.

little wooden horse standing on the deck and turned away.

"Anyone can have him who pleases," he said angrily, walking off.

Now all the other sailors began to quarrel over the little wooden horse, for many of them had children and thought he would make a fine present to take home.

"We'll draw lots for him!" one of them cried. So they drew lots, and the little wooden horse fell to the share of a man whom he did not like the looks of at all – a morose, dark, blackened sailor with rings in his ears. The crew called him Pirate Jacky.

He had no children, so the sailors were very angry that he should have won the prize.

"What are you going to do with it?" they asked.

"Never you mind what I'm going to do with it," replied Pirate Jacky, sticking closely to his winnings, and he carried the little wooden horse down below, where he locked him in his sea chest.

The little wooden horse was very unhappy.

He was glad enough to have been rescued from the

sea horses, but he did not like belonging to Pirate Jacky, whose sea chest was dark and damp.

Then the ship was not sailing in the direction he wanted to go. Instead of going from north to south, it was sailing from east to west, taking him who knows how many miles away from his dear Uncle Peder.

Another thing which worried him very much was the clamour which he heard through the porthole above Pirate Jacky's chest. Outside the sea horses were still charging the sides of the ship till it shook with their buffeting, and he could hear their shrill, piercing whinnies saying, "He thinks he has escaped us, but we'll get him yet! We'll get him yet! We'll catch him if we follow him all round the world!"

These words frightened the little wooden horse very much, so that he felt quite glad to be safely hidden away in Pirate Jacky's chest below deck.

The little wooden horse soon slept, he was so tired, but the sea horses followed the ship all night. Sometimes they were quite silent, plunging in and out of the waves with easy flicks of their silver fins and tails, but towards morning they began to neigh again, waking the little wooden horse with their wild, shrill clamour. He lay trembling, hoping that Pirate Jacky would not open the box until they had gone away.

Pirate Jacky left him in the sea chest the whole of that day, but at nightfall the sea horses were still following the boat. They were wilder now than ever, battering at the timbers till the vessel shuddered and leapt and rolled. On deck the men were busy, for they expected a bad night.

"Look at that!" they said, as the sea horses flung themselves against the prow more fiercely than before. "We shall have trouble before dawn."

About midnight the little wooden horse, who had been listening for hours to the gathering storm, felt the ship give a sudden heave, and then roll over so violently that the sea chest slid across the floor and crashed violently into the opposite beams. The next moment a second violent roll sent it back again, and thenceforward it could not lie still, but was rolled, shoved, rocked, and buffeted across the planks, till only the strong iron corners and lock kept it together.

"This is terrible!" said the little wooden horse, who was considerably bruised all over. He began to wish Pirate Jacky would come and let him out.

Pirate Jacky did not come, and things went from bad to worse.

The sea chest was pitched on end, turned completely over, rocked violently from side to side, as the ship swayed, yawed, and wallowed in the teeth of the storm. The noise was terrible. There was the wind in the rigging, and such a wind as had never been heard. There was the hissing scream of the rain, the shatter of thunder, the clattering roar and tumble of the waves. In and out of all the other noises the sailors shouted to one another, the timbers of the ship creaked and moaned, and the sea horses whinnied their excitement, while in Pirate Jacky's sea chest the little wooden horse sobbed. "Oh, dear! Oh, dear! What an unlucky little fellow I am! Here I am, a quiet little horse that only wishes to return and stay for ever by his master's side, rescued from the jaws of the terrible sea horses only to be battered to death in the storm!"

Soon the racket and the rocking were too tremendous for him to sob or to think any longer. The little wooden horse could no longer tell if he were standing on his head or his heels. The noise was so deafening he thought he must die, when all of a sudden there came the loudest crack he had ever heard in his life. With a desperate shiver the ship stood still – then with one terrible downward plunge she dived to her doom, and the little wooden horse felt the water rushing about the hold.

Now he knew he was no longer resting on planks, for he could feel the water lapping about the corners of the box. He was gently bobbing in it, but whether he was on the surface of the sea or sunk with the ship miles below the ocean he could not tell. The water did not come inside the chest, and the bobbing, floating motion was much quieter and more pleasant than the terrible racketing he had suffered before.

Suddenly he heard the sailors' voices in the water close to him, together with the splash of oars.

"Is everyone in the lifeboats?" they shouted to one another.

"Everyone except Pirate Jacky," somebody said, and they all began shouting for Pirate Jacky.

There was no answer, although the two boats rowed several times around the sinking ship, with the sailors calling his name. Whether the noise of the storm drowned their voices or not they could not tell. Pirate Jacky never answered.

"He's gone!" one of the sailors shouted. "Better row away!"

"What's that?" another cried. "A sea chest to starboard!"

"That's Pirate Jacky's chest!" a third sailor called. "Better let it go with the poor fellow!"

The little wooden horse could not believe that he would be left behind, locked up in Pirate Jacky's sea chest, but as the sailors' voices died away in the howling of the storm he saw that it really was so: he was to be left all alone, tossed up and down by the tremendous waves in the middle of the ocean. The little wooden horse did not like this idea at all.

Then, as the sailors' voices faded quite away, he heard the sea horses once more. They had hushed their shrill neighing as the ship split in half, a little awed by the disaster they had caused; but now they were prancing about the floating timbers, snuffling, peering inquisitively into everything they saw.

"Where is it – the funny creature that called itself a horse?" they whinnied. "It must be somewhere. Presently it will come to the surface, and we can catch it again!"

The little wooden horse was very relieved when the waves carried the chest farther and farther away from the wreck, around which the eager little sea horses snuffled and pried. Presently he could not hear their high voices any more.

"This is better," said the little wooden horse, picking up heart. "After all, in several days' time I may be cast up on some shore where the people will be kind to me, and will help me to get back to my dear master, Uncle Peder, in the forest."

Now the little wooden horse did not know it, but some of the big wooden spars had floated a long way from the wreck. One of these was close beside Pirate Jacky's sea chest, and presently the sea flung them together with a *thud!* that awakened the little wooden horse, who had just dozed off to sleep.

To his dismay he saw a stream of water rushing in at the corner of the chest, for the blow had shattered the lid.

The little wooden horse flung himself against the lid and pushed with all his might. It gave way without much trouble, for the night's battering had weakened the whole chest. The little wooden horse shot to the surface like a cork.

After two nights and a day in the chest his eyes were so blinded that at first he could tell neither the time of day or night, nor where the sea ended and the sky began. Then he saw that a grey dawn was breaking over the stormy sea; there was no horizon anywhere to be seen, but the waves were dying down, and only a splash or two of silver far behind him told where the sea horses still played and pried about the wreck of the ship.

Glad to be free again, the little wooden horse began to swim with all his might in what he hoped was the right direction.

Presently the sun came up, which cheered him

very much. The waves died down, and in a clear blue sea he swam and rested by turns, certain that by nightfall at least he must reach the farther shore.

He had not swum more than an hour when he saw in the water near him something dark floating.

"It looks very like a man!" said the little wooden horse curiously, swimming up close to see. What was his astonishment when he looked down into the black beard and closed eyes of Pirate Jacky!

The little wooden horse laid his head against the sailor's chest to see if he were drowned; but no, he could hear his heart beating faintly within, like the ticking of a clock that was nearly run down.

The little wooden horse was not very fond of Pirate Jacky, who had treated him roughly and left him locked up two nights and a day in a sea chest, where he might have been drowned if it had not been for the timber that had shattered the lid.

"But I cannot leave him here to drown," said the little wooden horse. "I must take him with me." So he took Pirate Jacky's coat gently between his wooden teeth and began to swim with him.

The sailor was a heavy man: the little wooden horse found that he could swim only very slowly, carrying such a weight in his teeth.

"Never mind," he said. "Sooner or later we shall reach the shore, and if it is a little sooner or a little later, what does it matter?"

By and by the little wooden horse discovered that he would never reach any shore by nightfall, if he ever did at all. Pirate Jacky was so heavy it was all he could do to swim twenty yards without resting.

"Now why do I feel so heavy and tired?" said the little wooden horse to himself.

Then he thought of all the money inside his little wooden body, and how heavily it weighed him down.

"If I threw away some of those pennies, which are not, after all, worth very much," said the little wooden horse, "I should be much lighter, and then I could swim better and faster."

So he took off his little wooden head and threw away some of the pennies that he had earned on the seashore, after which he was able to swim much faster and to carry Pirate Jacky with a firmer grip.

When he had swum half a mile farther Pirate Jacky opened his eyes. He was surprised enough to see the little wooden horse swimming along, holding his coat between his wooden teeth.

"Well, now I think I can swim a little by myself," said Pirate Jacky, so the little wooden horse let go of him thankfully enough. But after a few hundred yards the sailor was in trouble again, and the little wooden horse once more had to swim for the two of them.

"Now this can't be done while I have such a weight in my inside," said the little wooden horse; so he took off his head and threw the rest of the pennies into the sea.

Pirate Jacky opened his eyes when he saw the money thrown away, but he said nothing, for he was a man who minded his own business.

By and by he closed his eyes again, for he was very weak and faint, and his body weighed more and more heavily upon the strength of the little wooden horse.

"I really cannot swim much better unless I throw away some more of the coins that are inside my body," said the little wooden horse, looking anxiously into Pirate Jacky's closed eyes. So he bravely took off his wooden head and threw five of his precious silver coins into the sea.

So they swam on, but every now and then the little wooden horse had to take off his wooden head and throw one, two, or three more coins into the ocean, till his little body was so light he dared not think about it. But his strength was still ebbing away.

Pirate Jacky lay a dead weight between his wooden teeth. The sailor's black eyes were closed; his black beard was entangled in his gold earrings. The little wooden horse hoped he was not dead.

"And yet what does it matter?" he said sorrowfully to himself. "We shall both die before long. There is no land within reach, and my strength is nearly gone."

Suddenly, ahead of them, he saw land!

At first the little wooden horse could not believe his eyes for joy, but then he saw that there really were trees ahead of him, and a tiny hill. Was it possible that they had come at last to the other side of the ocean?

He began to swim with all his might, but for all his courage the land seemed to get no nearer, and he flung away coin after coin to make his body lighter and better able to carry his own weight and that of Pirate Jacky.

At last, when the moon rose once more and the first stars twinkled over the sea, the little wooden horse reached the shore, still carrying Pirate Jacky bravely between his wooden teeth. He had thrown away his last coin, and was almost too feeble to struggle up the sand. When at last he felt his four wooden wheels on firm, dry ground once more the little wooden horse dropped the sailor on the sand, and fell down himself to sleep a heavy sleep that lasted till far into the next day.

"When the morning comes," was his last waking thought, "I will set out through the forest to find Uncle Peder."

17 PIRATE JACKY AND BILL BLACKPATCH

WHEN THE LITTLE WOODEN HORSE opened his eyes the next morning to find the hot sun above him, the warm sand below him, the birds singing, the waves lapping gently a few yards away, and not a vestige of a silver sea horse to be seen, he felt so happy that he laid back his ears and kicked his hind wheels high in the air.

When he remembered that he had swum the whole way across the ocean he neighed with joy, and even the thought of his lost fortune could not damp his spirits. He could not bear to wait another moment before taking the road back through the forest to Uncle Peder, so he looked round for Pirate Jacky to say goodbye.

Pirate Jacky had lighted a fire to dry his clothes. He was sitting beside it, gazing solemnly out to sea.

"Why, where are you going?" he asked the little wooden horse when he came up to say goodbye.

"Home through the forest, of course!" said the little wooden horse joyfully.

Pirate Jacky stared at him, and then chuckled.

"You've a long way to go before you get home, my little wooden horse," he said, not unkindly. "Do you really want to swim again so soon? Don't you know that this is not the other side of the ocean, but a little island in the middle of the sea? I know it well, for I have been here before."

When the little wooden horse heard Pirate Jacky's words he thought his wooden heart would break. He followed the sailor along the shore till they had walked round the whole island, when he saw that it was indeed true. It was only a very small island after all; there was nothing to be seen on either side but water.

"Never mind," said Pirate Jacky when he saw the tears pouring out of the painted eyes of the little wooden horse. "Perhaps, after all, you will be glad one day that you came to this island. For I am going to reward you for saving my life. Come with me."

Trying hard to control his sobs, the little wooden horse followed Pirate Jacky up the steep rocks of the little hill in the centre of the island. Through bushes and long, thick grass they stumbled and pushed their way, till they came out of the trees, and when they were nearly at the top Pirate Jacky dived into a cranny between two rocks.

"Follow me!" he told the little wooden horse.

The little wooden horse followed Pirate Jacky down the cranny till they came to a flat rock at the end. This rock was marked with a cross. Pirate Jacky pushed the rock with his hand, and it swung back into darkness.

"Whatever can this be?" thought the little wooden horse when he saw Pirate Jacky squeeze through the space and disappear inside the mountain. He felt as though he were going down the mines again, but he did not want to be left behind, so he squeezed through the crack after Pirate Jacky, and found himself in an enormous cave.

Inside the cave the little wooden horse blinked, gasped, and rubbed his painted eyes in astonishment.

The blue stripes on his round little body paled with wonder, while his four wooden wheels set up such a tremble and rattle of excitement that Pirate Jacky turned round and sharply told him to be quiet.

For all about the cave, in piles and heaps, in caskets, in crates, and in boxes, was such a treasure as the little wooden horse had never dreamed of. Piles of golden coins, sparkling jewels, emeralds, pearls, rubies, diamonds – all flashing out of the darkness at the little wooden horse, winking at him with their sparkling eyes, saying, "Take us! Fill yourself with us! We are yours!"

Pirate Jacky nodded to the little wooden horse to help himself. The sailor sat down on a cask and gazed around the treasure chamber, while the little wooden horse without more ado whipped off his head and scuttled round the golden heaps, picking here diamonds, there pearls, there golden coins, till his little body was filled to bursting point, and he felt so rich he could hardly contain himself. How Uncle Peder's eyes would pop out of his head at the sight of such a fortune! They would never be in want again!

Piles of golden coins . . . emeralds, pearls, rubies . . .

Pirate Jacky sat smiling kindly as the little wooden horse crammed himself with treasure, and told him to go on till he could carry no more.

"You will never get such a chance again," said he. "Only one more fellow knows of this cave, and that's a rascally sailor called Bill Blackpatch, who is no friend of mine. We found it together when we were on the same ship, a long while ago, and stopped at this island for water. We didn't want to tell the rest of the crew about it, or to be seen with diamonds and pearls in our pockets, so we left it alone; but each of us vowed we would come back one day and collect the treasure before the other could get at it. Then we signed on different ships, and till yesterday I have not been able to return to the island. I have lain awake at night thinking of Blackpatch coming back and stealing the treasure from under my nose, so when the ship went down I decided to dodge the lifeboats and swim for the island, which I knew was hereabouts. As you know, my strength gave out quickly, and if it had not been for you, my little wooden horse, I would never have arrived at all.

When I opened my eyes and found myself on the shore last night, and saw you asleep beside me, I staggered up the hill to this cave to see if Bill Blackpatch had been here before me. Luckily for me he has not, so you and I will make our fortunes. I mean to cut down trees, and make a boat and enough boxes to hold all the treasure safely. Then, when a fine day comes and we are ready, we will row across to the farther shore, and then if you wish it, my little wooden horse, we can part company, and you can take your part of the treasure back to your Uncle Peder."

The little wooden horse was overjoyed with this idea. He promised to help his utmost with the making of the boat and the chests, so that they would soon be ready to carry the treasure away across the sea. Pirate Jacky and the little wooden horse worked night and day making the boat and the chests. Pirate Jacky cut down trees; the little wooden horse dragged them to the shore and went back for more. He knocked in the pegs with his strong wooden wheels, and was more useful than ten sailors.

Presently they had made a beautiful brown boat,

called the *Treasure Trove*, and two strong oars with which to row her. Pirate Jacky cut down more trees with his sailor's knife, and made twelve strong chests, which the little wooden horse carried down to the boat.

Then they had to fill them with the treasure – they were too heavy to carry up and down the mountain when they were full – so the little wooden horse emptied himself of his own fortune, which he hid carefully in the prow of the boat, and scuttled up and down, filling his little wooden body from the heaps in the cave, and taking the treasure thus down to the shore to be emptied into the chests. Pirate Jacky did the same thing, filling his pockets, his boots, and his red cap with the coins and jewels on his journeys up and down.

Presently the cave was empty, but all the chests were full. On the rocky door at the end of the cranny Pirate Jacky wrote, "Pirate Jacky, his mark", with the picture of a dagger, as a sign for Bill Blackpatch when he should come.

Underneath the little wooden horse drew the

picture of a wheel, with "The little wooden horse, his mark", because he thought it looked fine and daring.

Now Pirate Jacky had to make lids for the chests, and strong pegs to peg them down.

The little wooden horse dreamed day and night of the surprise he was going to bring to Uncle Peder. One day, when the lids were nearly finished, the little wooden horse saw the sailor, as he thought, some way off among the trees.

"Pirate Jacky! Pirate Jacky!" he cried to make himself known, but to his surprise the sailor immediately began to run, and soon disappeared into the wood.

By and by, when they met upon the shore, the little wooden horse, very puzzled, asked, "Why did you run away from me in the woods just now, Pirate Jacky, when I called out to you among the trees?"

Pirate Jacky looked at him in great surprise.

"Why, my little wooden horse, I wouldn't run away from you! And I wasn't in the woods just now. I was up on the mountain cutting pegs."

"Well, that is funny," said the little wooden horse, "for I felt sure I saw you – red cap, blue coat, and all!"

"You must have dreamed it, my little wooden horse," said Pirate Jacky.

Now the chests were finished, and until the moon rose they worked hard loading the boat, for the weather was fine, and they meant to start the next day. The little wooden horse went to bed so happy he could scarcely sleep.

But when they went down to the shore in the morning what should they find but a great hole in the bottom of the boat – a hole that had not been there when they went to bed!

"Oh, dear! Oh, dear! How unfortunate we are!" cried Pirate Jacky. "The tide lifted the boat in the night and dashed her on a rock. Now we shall not be able to start till I have mended it, and that will take me three whole days!"

He set to work directly, while the little wooden horse fetched and carried, and made himself as useful as he knew how.

When he had done all he could and Pirate Jacky

was still at work the little wooden horse wandered round the island, saying goodbye to his favourite places, for after all he had worked hard and been very happy there.

He was wandering down the shore at the far end of the island when something under the bushes of a tiny creek caught his painted eye. He went up to see what the strange object could be, pushed away under the bushes as though somebody wanted to hide it. It was a boat!

The little wooden horse examined the boat all over very curiously. It was green, with two green oars, and it looked as though it had been used quite lately.

"Now whoever can it belong to?" wondered the little wooden horse, trundling pensively back along the shore.

When he reached Pirate Jacky's side he found the sailor had finished mending the boat. Everything was ready to start the next day.

The little wooden horse decided to say nothing about the strange little green boat that he had found, but to keep a sharp look out all that night. So he never closed his painted eyes at all, but lay with his wooden ears a-prick, his attention fixed on the seashore.

Just before dawn he heard a slight noise outside, near the boat, as though somebody were trying to walk very silently, carrying something heavy at the same time.

The little wooden horse got up quietly, and trundled down to the shore to see what could be happening.

There he saw a very strange thing – Pirate Jacky in his red cap and blue jersey carrying chest after chest away from the *Treasure Trove* and dumping it in the little green boat, which was pulled up on the shore a few yards away.

"Now that is a very funny thing!" said the little wooden horse. "For whatever can Pirate Jacky want with two boats? And why did he hide the first and say nothing about it? And why is he putting away all the chests that we packed so carefully into the green boat? Does he mean to go away in the dark and leave me behind?"

But at that moment the sailor turned round, and

the little wooden horse saw that it was *not* Pirate Jacky after all, in spite of his red cap and blue jersey, but a sailor with a black patch over one eye and a big red moustache!

This strange sailor did not see the little wooden horse: he was far too busy taking the chests out of the brown boat and putting them into the green one.

The little wooden horse hurried back up the shore, and soon found Pirate Jacky asleep and snoring under a bush.

"Pirate Jacky! Pirate Jacky! Wake up!" he told him. "A strange sailor has come and is stealing all the treasure!"

Pirate Jacky was up in a moment and running down to the shore, where the strange sailor had just lifted the last chest out of the *Treasure Trove* and was struggling with it towards his own little green boat.

"Bill Blackpatch!" roared Pirate Jacky.

"Pirate Jacky!" shouted the other sailor, dropping the chest in his fright, and they fell upon each other like two wolves.

The little wooden horse had never seen such a fight. He kept well out of the way as the two punched and tore and bit and buffeted at each other. The sand flew in all directions. Now they wallowed in the sea, trying to push each other into deep water, now they struggled far up the shore; and all the while their shouts and arguments could have been heard from the other side of the island.

"The treasure is mine, I tell you! I came first!"

"But we found it together!"

"I claimed it!"

"I claimed it too! It's mine, not yours!"

"*Yours!* It belongs to me, I tell you!"

As there was nothing else he could do while he waited for them to stop, the little wooden horse made himself busy fetching the chests from Bill Blackpatch's boat and putting them back into the *Treasure Trove*. When he had fetched six, however, he became thoughtful, and carried no more.

The two sailors fought until the sun rose, when they were so sore and bruised and battered that by common consent they agreed to stop and rest for a little while before going on. But they did not stop arguing, each claiming that the treasure was his alone, although neither of them had any good reason for saying so.

At last the little wooden horse could bear it no longer.

"Oh, my dear sirs," he began, "I know I am only a little wooden horse, and a quiet one, and I do not like quarrelling at all. But it seems to me that the treasure belongs as much to Bill Blackpatch as it does to Pirate Jacky, and as much to Pirate Jacky as it does to Bill, seeing that you both found it together at the same time. Now with six chests each you will both make your fortunes ten times over, and I suggest that we get into our different boats with six chests each aboard and row away wherever we will, for, as for myself, I am very anxious to find my way back to my dear master, Uncle Peder, and stay for ever at his side."

When the two pirates heard this very sensible argument they agreed at last to do as the little wooden horse had said, so they picked themselves up off the sand and got into their boats, each with six chests; and while Bill Blackpatch rowed round the back of the island and away over the sea from where he had come, Pirate Jacky and the little wooden horse left the island behind and rowed in the direction that they believed the farther shore to be.

18 THE LITTLE WOODEN HORSE GOES HOME

PIRATE JACKY ROWED FOR A NIGHT and a day, till at last they reached the shore of which the little wooden horse had dreamed for so long. His wooden heart beat fiercely with excitement when the boat touched the shore and he found himself quite close to the port where he had begun his journey across the ocean with the elephant so long ago.

"Well, I am sorry that we are to part, my little wooden horse," said Pirate Jacky when they stood side by side on firm ground. "Good luck to your journeys! Perhaps we shall meet again one day!"

"Perhaps we shall," said the little wooden horse, though he did not think it likely, for he meant to stay by Uncle Peder's side for ever and ever. However, he wished Pirate Jacky good luck and farewell, waved his wooden legs in turn, and trundled away to find the road by the canal that would lead him home.

He avoided the port this time: he did not want the sailors to play any more tricks on him, lifting him high up in the air on cranes and setting him down on strange ships that took him over the sea, away from Uncle Peder. So he trundled round the outside of the port till he came to the canal, and there he set out along the towpath that he remembered so well from his race to the port many long months ago.

The little wooden horse was happy as he hurried along. His wooden body was crammed too full of treasure even to rattle, but his four wooden wheels made a cheerful noise that was pleasant to hear.

Presently he saw ahead of him a familiar sight – a great barge that had finished its business in the port swinging up the canal, towed by a strong black horse on the bank. The little wooden horse's heart warmed as he saw it, and he thought of the great race he had run with the *Marguerita* and Farmer Max behind him.

He had never seen the black horse before, but something about the lines of the barge made him look and look again to make certain – for it was – it was – the *Marguerita*!

The little wooden horse quickened his pace, till he was trundling along side by side with the big black horse, and all of a sudden there came a cry from the people on board the barge.

"See there! See! It's our little wooden horse!"

The horse drew the *Marguerita* close in to the bank, and in a moment the little wooden horse was on board among his friends of the canal, who were all talking at once, all petting him and asking him questions.

"What happened to you that day?" they asked. "We waited for you all that evening, and the next, but you never came. Every journey we have made since we have searched the whole port for you, but nobody could tell us where you had gone."

They insisted on paying him the money they had owed him, and although the little wooden horse was rich now, he did not like to hurt their feelings by refusing to accept it. So instead he gave the barge man's wife a very beautiful sparkling ruby, and she cried with joy at receiving such a handsome present.

The little wooden horse offered to go and help the black horse pull the barge, but the barge people would not hear of it.

"You must ride with us this time," they insisted, "and tell us all your adventures. Besides, that is the strongest horse on the river. We bought him with the money we got for the timber the day you pulled the *Marguerita* first into port. He never tires."

So the little wooden horse stayed with the barge people and told them his adventures, till they were far up the canal and his road to the forest branched away through the fields out of sight of the canal.

There he said goodbye to his friends, and asked them whether, if Uncle Peder should send a load of wooden horses to be sold across the sea, the *Marguerita* would very kindly see them down the canal and put them safely on to a ship in the port.

The barge people promised they would do this without fail, so the black horse drew them away up the towpath, while the little wooden horse struck out across the fields towards the forest.

"How pleasant this is, to be going home to my dear master with such treasure!" said the little wooden horse.

He trundled all through the night, and in the morning found himself on roads that he remembered very well.

"Why," said the little wooden horse, "I must be quite close beside Farmer Max's farm! Yes! Here are the fields I trundled through on my way to the canal. There is the ditch I hid in, and heard him go galloping by. And there – yes, there is the farm itself – more tumbledown than ever, with holes in all the roofs!

"What a poor little fellow I was then!" said the little wooden horse. "So scared and bullied and afraid, with scarcely a penny to my name! Now that I am going home full of riches I am not afraid any more. I almost believe I feel brave enough to have a look round the farm and risk meeting Farmer Max himself."

So saying, the little wooden horse left the safe high road and trundled into Farmer Max's farm.

The ducks in the pond saw him first. They stood on their heads and waved their feet at him. The little wooden horse prowled round the corners he remembered best.

There were the heavy hay carts he used to pull, more battered than ever, with their wheels falling off. There was the lane to the fields, with even deeper ruts and puddles in it than he remembered. There was the little shed in which he had been locked many and many a night, and where he had fallen asleep, tired and miserable, dreaming of Uncle Peder.

"I must go and see if the hole is still there that I made," said the little wooden horse, creeping inside the shed where he had once slept.

He had hardly entered the shed before there came a tramping in the yard of heavy feet, and a loud voice that the little wooden horse knew very well and trembled in spite of himself to hear. It was Farmer Max ordering the men out into the fields.

At the same time the ducks bobbed their heads up out of the water and sang derisively, "Quaack! Quaack! Quaack! What about the little wooden horse?"

When Farmer Max threw a stone at them they

ducked their heads under the water again, waving their feet at him.

Farmer Max strode round the farm to make sure that all the horses were out and none of the men were missing.

"Little wooden horse, indeed!" he was muttering. "If I ever catch that little horse again I'll never let him go."

The little wooden horse trembled as he heard the farmer go striding by. He hid under the manger where he used to feed, but nobody came in.

For all that he did not want to stay another moment in the place, and when Farmer Max had gone he galloped out of the shed as quickly as his wheels would carry him.

He dared not cross the yard to the gate in the open in case he should be seen, so he began to creep in and out of the sheds, always getting nearer and nearer to the gate, and trying to make himself invisible.

"That was very unpleasant!" said the little wooden horse, as he trundled round the back of the farthest barn. "I was a very foolish little horse to risk such danger." And he was turning the corner to bolt through the gate when whom should he meet face to face but – Farmer Max!

The little wooden horse froze stiff with terror as he found himself once more in front of the tyrant who had treated him so badly.

"Now I am lost for ever!" said the little wooden horse, and a sob rose in his throat as he thought of his dear Uncle Peder whom he would now never see again.

What was his astonishment when Farmer Max walked straight past him, almost knocking him over, as if he had not seen him at all!

For some time after he had passed the little wooden horse stood motionless, trembling with fear, not able to believe in his good fortune.

Then he made a dash for the gate, and was off down the highway like a flash, not daring to look behind him for fear he should see the angry farmer hot upon his trail.

But nobody followed him, and after a while the little wooden horse slackened his pace, while his breath became calmer and his heart beat less violently inside his wooden body.

"I am a very lucky little horse," he whispered to himself. "I am luckier than I deserve for being so reckless."

He trundled along till midday, when he paused to rest by a hayfield where some other horses were working. To his delight he recognized them as his companions at Farmer Max's haymaking, and they knew him at once, running up to him to ask his news.

When he had told them his adventures the little wooden horse explained his last visit to Farmer Max, and how he had passed quite close to the farmer without being seen at all.

"Oh, that is not surprising!" said the horses. "Farmer Max never sees anything nowadays. His meanness has made him so short-sighted that unless he is wearing his spectacles he is nearly blind."

The horses wished the little wooden horse much luck and happiness as he set out again, and soon he was alone once more, with afternoon shadows running to meet him out of the forest that now loomed up to welcome him back.

"Truly I am a very lucky little horse," said the little wooden horse.

He walked all day, and slept the night in the forest. The next day found him still trundling along, a little tired, but very happy, till he passed the white house where the little girl lived who had first loved him.

"I know it is foolish," said the little wooden horse, hesitating at the gate instead of passing by, "but I should like to take another peep into that playhouse, and see if the little girl is still there, and if it is all as fine and splendid as I remember when I went away."

So he pushed open the gate and trotted inside. The big house was quiet, just as before, while down the garden the apple trees had not changed a twig. The playhouse under the trees had had a new coat of green paint, but the door was open, just as it had been the first day the little wooden horse found it.

This time he did not trundle round and round the house. He went straight up to the playhouse

He walked all day, and slept the night in the forest.

door and peeped through the chink, meaning to run away in a moment should the rocking horse open his mouth.

But the rocking horse was quite still today, his dignity gone, his paint cracked and scratched. He stood drooping his head, with an old cocked hat over one of his broken ears.

On the floor, looking as fresh and dainty as ever, the little girl sat rather sadly mending some torn picture books.

Although the little wooden horse made no sound, something made her look up, and in a moment she had sprung to her feet, and was smothering him with kisses and reproaches.

"Oh! Oh! My dear, my darling, my naughty little wooden horse! Why have you been away so long? Why haven't you sent me that new, beautiful wooden horse like yourself that your master was to make for me? Where have you been all this time? I've been so lonely, so they sent for my boy cousins to play with me; but they spoiled my rocking horse and scratched my toys and tore my picture books.

I didn't want them. I only want a dear little wooden horse like you to play with."

The little wooden horse told of all his adventures as soon as he was allowed to speak a word for himself, and the little girl listened, her eyes growing rounder and rounder with horror and wonder as he told of all the things he had done. Most of all she wanted to hear about the ten little Princes and Princesses who were going to have ten little wooden horses just like the one that Uncle Peder was going to make for herself.

"And now you mustn't stop one *minute*. You must go back to him," she said, pushing the little wooden horse out of the playhouse door. "But one day you must come back and see me, and tell me your adventures all over again."

The little wooden horse promised that he would do so, and then he trundled away through the forest with his heart bounding higher and higher with happiness the nearer he got to Uncle Peder.

The hours went by, but he was no longer tired. Every path, every tree, looked friendly now, and he did not stop to sleep or feed.

So the next day, when the sun was high in the sky, the little wooden horse came to the last bit of forest before the little old woman's shed.

"By now Uncle Peder will have told her about me," he said to himself. "She will be kind to me, and perhaps she will be sorry that she threw me into the cabbage bed. I think Uncle Peder himself will be sitting in the sun outside the cottage door, and there will be a little curl of blue smoke coming out of the chimney where the little old woman is cooking the midday dinner. I shall trundle up to the cottage door and say, 'Hello, Uncle Peder, my dear master!' Just like that! 'Here I am! Here is your little wooden horse come back from seeking his fortune, with enough money for us both to live on for ever and ever!'"

He passed the last trees, the last rocks. In a moment he would be there.

"Now I shall shut my eyes and go on while I count fifty," said the little wooden horse. "When I open them again I shall be round the corner, and the little cottage will be there before me, with Uncle Peder sitting outside the door, just as I have seen it so often in my dreams."

So the little wooden horse trundled on, counting fifty as he went, till he had turned the corner and was in the well-remembered glade.

"Now I will open my eyes!" said the little wooden horse.

He opened them wide and looked about him; but now they grew round with surprise and fear, for there was no cottage in front of him, no blue smoke coming out of the chimney, no cabbage patch, no Uncle Peder sitting before the door, no shed, no garden, and no cow house!

Everything was in ruins, with the weeds rambling in and out of the bricks as though for a very long time there had been nobody there.

Uncle Peder was gone, and there was no sign of him to be seen anywhere.

19 THE LITTLE WOODEN HORSE
GOES TO A WEDDING

THE LITTLE WOODEN HORSE spent the night among the ruins of the cottage. His wooden heart was heavy with misery; he was too wretched even to cry. The treasure that rattled inside his wooden body did not comfort him at all, for he had collected it for Uncle Peder, and without Uncle Peder the little wooden horse preferred to die.

The next day he rose heavily from his uncomfortable bed and wandered into the forest, not because he thought he would have any luck there, but because he had nowhere else to go.

So the little wooden horse began his travels again, trundling through the forest by day, sleeping under the trees by night, hoping against hope that one day he would see or hear something of the dear master he had lost.

Now and then he passed through villages where, a long while ago, he had followed Uncle Peder selling his wooden toys.

At these villages the little wooden horse stopped and asked, "Oh, please, have you seen a poor old man passing by lately – Uncle Peder by name?"

But the people always shook their heads and said they had never heard of such a fellow.

"Then perhaps you have seen a little old woman driving a little brown cow?" the little wooden horse persisted; but the people always shook their heads and said they had seen no strangers at all.

By and by he came to the end of the forest, beyond which stretched a plain wider than any he knew, with villages, towns, churches, and farms belonging to strange people who spoke a new language.

"Surely Uncle Peder would not leave the forest he knows so well?" thought the little wooden horse, gazing out across the new country, which looked so vast and strange he did not want to set foot in it at all.

So he turned about and trundled back the way he had come, but choosing new paths, and always hoping to hear news of Uncle Peder on the way.

At last, when he had worn his paint to a mere scratch of colour, and even the strong iron bands that bound his wheels were wearing thin, the little wooden horse came once more into the glade where the cottage had stood, and now he did not know what to do or where to go, or what had become of his dear master, Uncle Peder.

So he sat down again on the old pile of stones and began to cry large, fat tears out of his painted eyes.

"I am so lonely!" sobbed the little wooden horse, who thought that at last his heart was really broken.

There was plenty of company in the glade that morning, however, although nobody noticed the little wooden horse. People in their best clothes were hurrying past the ruined cottage on their way to the forest church, whose joyful bells could be heard through the trees inviting everybody to come and join in the wedding.

Children ran by carrying flowers, old men limped

along on sticks, young women hurried past fastening their ribbons – everyone was going in the same direction, and for the moment the whole forest was alive with their talk and laughter and bright wedding clothes.

When they had gone the glade seemed lonelier than ever, while the little wooden horse was tired enough of his own company.

"I think I shall go after them and see what is happening in the church," said the little wooden horse, rising from the pile of stones and plodding on his broken wheels in the same direction as everyone else had gone.

When he arrived at the church all the guests were already inside, for the wedding had begun, but outside an argument was going on between the driver of the wagonette that was to take the bride and bridegroom to their new home and the owner of the horse, who was insisting that he had only been paid to bring them to church.

In vain the driver insisted that money had been paid for both journeys, that the bride and bridegroom were poor, and that anyway it had all been settled before. The owner of the horse would not listen to him, and when he found out that not another penny was to be had he unharnessed his horse and led him away, while the driver wrung his hands and stamped up and down in despair, calling himself the most unfortunate of drivers, and wondering what on earth the bride and bridegroom were going to do.

The little wooden horse was very kind-hearted. He did not like to see anyone in distress, besides which he longed for company and liked to help people when he could. So he went gently up to the driver of the wagonette and offered to pull it for him.

"For I am a strong little horse, and a quiet one," he said, remembering how he had helped to pull the King's coach round and round the city.

The driver was so grateful that he had not yet finished his thanks when the little wooden horse was harnessed to the wagonette, by which time the bells were pealing again and the guests coming out of church.

The driver hastily backed the wagonette up to the

church door as the bride and bridegroom appeared, and although the little wooden horse could see nothing, for he was facing the wrong direction, he felt he was being very useful, and this warmed his lonely little wooden heart.

All the guests shouted and waved their handkerchiefs as the bride and bridegroom, side by side inside the wagonette, left the church at a spanking trot.

The driver cracked his whip, and the little wooden horse bowled merrily along, thinking how nice it was to work for somebody again, and to do good turns to people who could not help themselves.

But although he was a steady little horse, and a quiet one, and had seen a hundred strange things in his travels, so that he never expected to be taken by surprise again, the little wooden horse nearly fell over backwards when there came a long sigh from behind him in the wagonette and a voice that he knew asked, "Why, my dear good soul, what can be the matter with you to sigh like that on your wedding day?"

For the voice that replied was Uncle Peder's, and the bride and bridegroom whom he was driving to their new home were none other than Uncle Peder and the little old woman from the cottage in the wood!

"Well, well, well!" sighed Uncle Peder. "We all have our joys and our sorrows, I suppose!"

"Ah!" said the little old woman. "I know what you are thinking of. You are sighing for your friend the little wooden horse, whom I chased away so cruelly from my door when you were ill many months ago. You will never be happy till he is found."

"I shall never find him now," said Uncle Peder. "He would have come back long ago if he had been alive."

"How differently I would treat him if he were alive now!" wept the little old woman. "Oh! Oh! Oh! I shall never forgive myself for what I did that terrible day."

Now Uncle Peder had to comfort her, which he did by putting his arm about her shoulders and calling her his dear little old woman, his little old wife. He talked to her of the new house he had built for her with his own hands in the wood when hers had fallen down, and how they were going to live there, poor but happy, for the rest of their lives.

"Ah, but I know you will never be perfectly happy without your little wooden horse!" sobbed the little old woman.

All this while the little wooden horse could hardly contain himself for excitement. He frisked and hopped from one side of the road to the other, till the driver wondered if he had been wise to rely on a perfectly strange little horse, who might, after all, upset them all and leave them in a ditch.

So he was quite glad when they came in sight of the little wooden house that Uncle Peder had built in the wood for himself and the little old woman to live in.

The little wooden horse was glad too, for a thousand times on the journey he had nearly cried out, "Here I am, Uncle Peder! Here is your little wooden horse, alive and well!" But he kept his mouth tightly shut and waited till they had drawn up before the newly painted door.

There Uncle Peder put his hand in his pocket to give the driver a coin, while the little old woman ran into the house for a lump of sugar to give to the horse that had drawn the wagonette. Suddenly she threw up her hands with a scream that brought Uncle Peder running to her side.

"Uncle Peder! Uncle Peder! Come quickly and tell me if I have lost my senses – or *is* that your little wooden horse that I drove from my door so cruelly so many months ago?"

But now the little wooden horse could not stand still any longer. With a piercing whinny of joy he sprang out of the harness, dropped the shafts to the ground, and ran into Uncle Peder's arms.

Never had there been such a wedding feast! There was the little old woman bustling in and out with a dozen new dishes, each better than the last. There was Uncle Peder, almost too happy to eat, jumping up to kiss now his little old wife, now his little wooden horse – and the little wooden horse himself, at the end of all his troubles, gazing and gazing at his dear master with such affection in his painted eyes that the little old woman cried with joy to watch them both.

Never had there been such a wedding feast!

And when the good things were eaten and the table cleared the little wooden horse took off his head and poured out of his wooden body the treasure that he had found on Pirate Jacky's island – the diamonds, the rubies, the emeralds, the pearls, all sparkling and gleaming like a magnificent dream – while Uncle Peder and the little old woman, their eyes round with wonder, listened over and over again to the story of his adventures. There was enough money there to keep them wealthy for ever: to buy corn for the land, a new cow, cabbages for the cabbage patch, a hive of bees, clothes, wool, comforts of every kind, and, best of all, new wood and paint, so that Uncle Peder could begin his new horses – the first for the little girl, the rest to be sent over the sea to the ten little Princes and Princesses, the miner's boy, the circus master, the shopkeeper, and last of all five particularly strong ones for the five noisy children who had used the little wooden horse so roughly.

Oh, what joy the little wooden horse had brought to the old woman, and to his master, Uncle Peder, who could now make toys to his heart's content, but only for those children who pleased him, or for those who had none of their own!

"I shall never leave home again," said the little wooden horse, for the old woman too loved him now, and he was tired of travelling.

But in the long winter evenings, when the fire burned brightly on the hearth and the wind howled outside, while the little old woman bustled round the kitchen busy with pots and pans, and while Uncle Peder carved wooden legs and wooden heads and wooden bodies, and painted red saddles and blue stripes on his new horses, the little wooden horse, content in his own corner, would go over and over his adventures again in imagination, from Farmer Max to Pirate Jacky, from the King's coach to the last journey with the barge people up the canal.

"For I am a quiet little horse, and for ever after I shall be rather a dull one," said he. "But I shall always be the luckiest little horse in the world."

AUTHOR NOTE

WHEN URSULA MORAY WILLIAMS was a little girl, she and her twin sister Barbara were sent to bed so early that they used to tell each other stories to pass the time before they went to sleep. After their mother had taught them to read and write, they began to make books – writing new stories and illustrating them with coloured pictures – which they gave to each other at Christmas or on their birthday. They made these "anniversary books" every year until they were teenagers. When they grew up, Ursula became a writer and Barbara a painter, and they remained close – although Ursula lived in England and her sister in Iceland.

Their parents, who were at one time both teachers, gave the girls and their younger brother the happiest of childhoods. The house where they lived was a huge old mansion lit by oil lamps, with an entrance hall paved in marble and surrounded by glass cases full of stuffed birds and animals – foxes, owls, weasels, jays and a large golden pheasant. The house was crumbling, and Ursula remembers that for their lessons with a governess "we moved from room to room as the ceilings fell on us." But it was a wonderful place to play in (there was a church organ that had no keyboard but provided a perfect hiding-place) – and in the big park outside they had a much-loved pony and cart.

In 1928, when the twins were nearly seventeen (they were

born on 19th April 1911), they were sent to France for a year to live in a pastor's house in Annecy in the Alps. There they had to go to school – which they hated – but out of school they enjoyed every moment: swimming, climbing, skiing and picnicking in the beautiful countryside. Ursula describes this time as like living in a fairy tale. When they came home, both sisters enrolled at the Winchester College of Art, but, while Barbara thrived, Ursula dropped out after a year and decided to practise her writing at home. She was encouraged by her uncle, Stanley Unwin (who was the famous publisher of *The Hobbit*), and her first book, *Jean-Pierre*, a story set in the mountains of Annecy, was published in 1931 with her own illustrations. She remembers that the book cost just 2s 6d (12½ pence)!

In 1935 Ursula married Conrad Southey John (always called Peter after their marriage), the great-grandson of the poet Robert Southey. To him she dedicated her best-known story, *Adventures of the Little Wooden Horse*, written when she was expecting their first child, Andrew. It was published in 1938 by George G. Harrap, who asked his favourite artist, Joyce Lankester Brisley (the creator of Milly-Molly-Mandy) to illustrate it. One of the first reviewers, Eleanor Graham (the first editor of Puffin Books) wrote, "I believe this story will find a permanent place among books for six to nine year olds, and will be loved by generations of children."

Ursula went on to have three more sons – Hugh, Robin and Jamie – and to write over seventy books for children. "I write compulsively," she says. "During the war years I was cooking for ten of us but I *had* to write, just as my twin sister had to paint and design." Her husband died in 1974, but she still lives in the family farmhouse on Bredon Hill in Gloucestershire where she brought up her children so happily. Ursula has ten grandchildren and many great-grandchildren.